FIRST LESSONS IN A DANGEROUS GAME

"You have a very fine leg, my lord," said Amanda.

Viscount Hawksborough fixed her with an icy stare. "I do not think I can possibly have heard you right, Miss Amanda."

"I said you have a very fine leg."

"Indeed," said Hawksborough.

"And . . . and . . . your eyes are like . . . are like . . . sixpences," Amanda finished lamely.

"What about my left eyebrow?" inquired the Viscount.

"I was trying to flirt, my lord, because it is the thing to do," said Amanda. "But obviously I do not know the right way to go about it."

"Then you need lessons." He picked up her hand and held it lightly in his and smiled into her eyes. "I could teach you. . . ."

THE VISCOUNT'S REVENGE

SIGNET Regency Romances You'll Enjoy

The Viscount's Revenge

by
Marion Chesney

①

A SIGNET BOOK

NEW AMERICAN LIBRARY

TIMES MIRROR

NAL BOOKS ARE AVAILABLE AT QUANTITY DISCOUNTS WHEN USED TO
PROMOTE PRODUCTS OR SERVICES. FOR INFORMATION PLEASE WRITE
TO PREMIUM MARKETING DIVISION, THE NEW AMERICAN LIBRARY,
INC., 1633 BROADWAY, NEW YORK, NEW YORK 10019.

SIGNET TRADEMARK REG. U.S. PAT. OFF. AND FOREIGN COUNTRIES
REGISTERED TRADEMARK—MARCA REGISTRADA
HECHO EN CHICAGO, U.S.A.

SIGNET, SIGNET CLASSIC, MENTOR, PLUME, MERIDIAN and NAL BOOKS
are published by The New American Library, Inc.,
1633 Broadway, New York, New York 10019

First Printing, November, 1983

1 2 3 4 5 6 7 8 9

PRINTED IN THE UNITED STATES OF AMERICA

For my friend
Tom Fitzgerald

1

"It is not as if we *really* have anything to worry about," said Amanda Colby, examining a purple-stained finger which she had just pricked on a bramble bush.

"Not us," replied her twin, Richard, cheerfully. "I think we have gathered enough berries to supply jam for *years*, Amanda. Aunt Matilda should be back from the reading of the will by now."

Amanda plucked a few more berries and then straightened her slim back and looked out over the fields of Hardforshire, rolling brown autumn fields bordered with scarlet and gold trees. The sky was deepening to violet on the horizon and there was already a nip of early frost in the air. The difficulty about gathering berries, she thought, was that brambles grew in hedgerows, and hedgerows had muddy ditches thick with nettles at the foot of them. Her stockings felt damp inside her sodden half-boots and her faded blue velvet cloak seemed inadequate protection against the early-evening chill.

The sun had set. It was a peaceful and quiet October evening.

Smoke climbed straight up into the tranquil air from

cottage chimneys and hips and haws in the thick thorn hedges glowed with a brighter color in the gathering dusk.

"Then let us go," said Amanda, picking up her pail of berries. "I must confess, Richard, I am a trifle concerned over the outcome of Uncle's will. Mr. Brotherington is his heir, you know, and he does not like us one bit, nor does that new wife of his. If Uncle Arthur has left us to his tender mercies, we may find ourselves destitute."

"Fustian," said Richard, falling into step beside her on the country road. "He has paid Aunt Matilda the allowance for our keep since Mother and Father died. He will simply have stated in his will that the allowance is to continue. Things will go on as they always have done, you'll see."

"I hope so," said Amanda with a shiver. "It is cold. Let's hurry."

They walked rapidly together, each carrying a pail brimming with berries.

"However," said Amanda, suddenly slowing as the tall chimneys of their home, Fox End, came into view, "I cannot help, you know, Richard, sometimes feeling that perhaps it is a trifle hard if things *are* to go on as they have always done. The allowance provides us with food and shelter but little else. I am weary of maintaining the position of a lady and struggling day in and day out with the rigours of genteel poverty. It was fun when we were children, but now . . . Oh, it *does* seem hard when there is a hunt ball or an assembly and all we can do is stand and wave to the carriages going past because we have not the clothes to attend or a carriage to take us there."

"Pooh," said Richard. "These things do not matter to me, although sometimes I do feel left out. But I do not wish to pay empty compliments to some silly girl. I have my horse and my gun, and we *are* good friends as well as being twins, Amanda."

"Oh, yes . . . but . . ." Amanda left the sentence unfinished. How could she explain to her boisterous sports-loving brother about the novels she read which filled her head with dreams?

"At least Amanda is much too young to be thinking of marriage," Aunt Matilda would say.

Amanda had thought of love and marriage for quite some months now. But that road for any gently bred girl led only through the neighbourhood balls and assemblies.

They rounded a bend in the road and Richard pushed open the rusty iron gates which led into the short drive of Fox End.

Fox End was a small country house built in the days of Queen Anne. It was badly in need of repairs, although its bow-fronted windows, cheerful red brick walls, and tiled roof with its jumble of massive chimney stacks presented a comfortable, welcoming appearance.

The central doorway opened into the hall from which rose the main staircase, and, behind the staircase, another door led from the far end into the garden. There was a drawing room, a dining room, a morning room, and a study on the ground floor, and, in addition, there were kitchens front and back, pantries and china cupboards and a place for coal.

Upstairs there were five bedrooms and two small dressing rooms. The servants' rooms were in the attics, but it had been quite a while since servants had lived at Fox End.

A woman came weekly from the nearby town of Hember Cross to do rough cleaning, and a man from the village came every few days to tend the three acres of garden and to do any other outside work and repairs. But either Aunt Matilda or Amanda did the cooking, and Amanda did all the sewing and washing.

There was a carriage house at the back, and stables where in palmier days had stood a carriage and a gig and four horses. But now there were only Richard's rawboned hunter and Amanda's donkey, Bluebell.

The Colby twins' parents had both died when they were still babies. Mr. and Mrs. Colby had both become infected with cholera during a visit to London, a severe bout from which neither had recovered. They had been a spendthrift couple who had considered themselves immortal, and so they had left no money.

After their deaths, Amanda and Richard were brought up by the late Mrs. Colby's spinster sister, Matilda Pettifor. "Uncle Arthur" was, in fact, no relative. He was simply Arthur Cogswell, who had been a close friend of the late Mr. Colby. Since the Colby twins seemed to have no relatives who were prepared to aid them—other than Miss Pettifor, who had no money at all—Mr. Cogswell had offered them a small monthly allowance, had agreed to pay for Richard's schooling, and had given them the use of Fox End. Mr. Brotherington, his nephew, was his heir.

The cold stillness of the autumn evening hung in the shadowy corners of the house.

"Perhaps Aunt Matilda is not home yet," said Amanda, leading the way to the kitchen with her pail of berries.

"The house is very cold. At least we do not need to economise on wood."

She swung off her cloak and threw it over the back of a chair while Richard lit the kitchen fire. Amanda filled a heavy kettle and swung it on the idleback so that the bottom hung over the crackling flames.

"Now, Richard," she said, "we will light a fire in the morning room and have tea when Aunt Matilda gets back."

"I'm hungry," said Richard. "All that fresh air and exercise!"

"Well, come into the morning room with me and help me with the fire and then I shall fetch a cold collation for us both. I confess to feeling sharp set myself."

She lit a candle and led the way back through the hall, her diminutive shadow flying before Richard's larger one.

"First," said Amanda, opening the door of the morning room and observing the gathering darkness, "we need to have more light in here."

She lit a branch of candles on the mantelshelf with the one she was holding, and, hearing an exclamation of dismay from her brother, swung around.

Aunt Matilda was scrunched up into a pathetic ball in one of the two winged armchairs which flanked the fireplace. A damp handkerchief was held to her mouth and tears coursed silently down her cheeks.

Amanda knelt quickly down beside her while Richard cleared his throat in an embarrassed way and occupied himself with lighting the fire.

"The will," said Amanda. "It was the will, was it not? He has left us nothing."

Aunt Matilda gave a weary little sigh like that of a very tired child who has cried itself out, and said in a whisper, "He has left us the house."

"Ah, then," cried Amanda, sitting back on her heels. "I have it. Your nerves have merely been overset by the relief from the strain."

Aunt Matilda shook her head slowly while her enormous starched linen and lace cap bobbed from side to side. "The house, yes," she gasped. "But no money."

Richard swore an ungentlemanly oath and dropped a log on the fire.

Amanda put her thin red hands to her cheeks. "Are you sure?" she asked. "Are you so very sure, dear Aunt? Of what use is the house to us if we have no money to eat?" Her face cleared. "Oh, you *misunderstood*. Mr. Brotherington, Uncle's heir, has been given instructions to continue the allowance."

Again the great white cap dipped and bobbed. "It was all very clear," said Aunt Matilda faintly. "It was implied in the will that Mr. Brotherington should attend to our needs, but you know how he is. He affected not to hear. The lawyer, Mr. Macdonald, *did* venture to ask him if he would be continuing the allowance, and he simply turned away and affected to be deaf."

"Then how are we supposed to go on?"

"Sell the house," said Aunt Matilda weakly.

"Sell Fox End!" cried Richard. "And then what? The money from the sale cannot last the three of us forever. At least here we have some shooting and fishing and vegetables from the garden."

"There is to be no more shooting or fishing," wailed Aunt Matilda. "Mr. Brotherington was oh! so *harsh*.

He had already hired a score of gamekeepers and he said in a very loud voice that anyone caught poaching on his land would be hanged at best and transported at least, no matter who they were."

Amanda stood up. "We shall go and see him immediately."

"No," said Richard heavily. "I feared this would happen. He detests us. It was last year when he invited us all at Uncle's request to one of his soirées. He had invited Sir James Framington in the hope that Sir James would form a *tendre* for that wretched daughter of his, Priscilla. Only Sir James became a trifle foxed and paid court to *you*, Amanda. *We* know he was not at all serious, for you were but seventeen with your hair down, and although you are very well in your way, you are not precisely . . . well, *you* know."

"Yes," said Amanda sadly, "*I* know. If I were better favored, there would be hope that I could trap a rich suitor, but as it is . . ."

"What are we to *do*?" sobbed Aunt Matilda, her long pink nose twitching in distress.

"Well, we have just received the allowance, so we are all right for another month . . . perhaps two, if we scrimp and save," said Amanda, thinking furiously. "Richard, go and fetch that last bottle of brandy, and take off the kettle. I think this calls for a celebration."

"What kind of celebration do you call this?" said Richard gloomily, moving towards the door.

"Well, I am not blessed with beauty, but you have always said I am too clever by half. This is the first test. A little brandy to animate my brain, and you will see . . . we will come about."

"I want to go to sleep," said Aunt Matilda, holding

her handkerchief over her face. "I don't want to eat, I don't want to drink brandy, I want to go to sleep *now*."

Amanda sighed. Aunt Matilda fled even the small pinpricks of reality in sleep. She could sleep sixteen hours at a stretch without the aid of laudanum. Tonight was not the time to beg her to stay awake.

"Very well," she said gently. "Come, and I will help you upstairs. Richard," she said to her brother, who had just entered the room with the brandy, "fetch a hot brick from the kitchen to put at Aunt Matilda's feet. I will light the fire in her room."

Aunt Matilda fell asleep almost immediately once she had been put into a clean nightdress and tucked into bed.

Her face under the nightcap looked pinched and old. How old was Aunt Matilda? wondered Amanda. Fifty? Or had her timid life of genteel poverty made her look older than her years?

She picked up the candle and made her way downstairs again.

Amanda and Richard sat on either side of the fire and drank brandy and looked at each other gloomily.

They did not look alike, although they were twins.

Amanda Colby was small and wiry with a small bosom and a tiny waist. Her hair sprang out from her brow in a frizzy auburn cloud. Sometimes she tamed it into ringlets with the curling tongs, but it would soon start to spring out from its neat prison into a mass of frizz again. She had very large hazel eyes, gold flecked with green, and thick, curling sandy lashes tipped with gold. Her nose was short and straight and her mouth soft and vulnerable. But her thin face and quick intelligent expression gave her rather a foxy look and she turned her head sharply at each sound, putting it a little on one side like a wild animal wary of hunters.

With a different upbringing, with a schooling in how to flirt and how to charm to a nicety, she might perhaps have achieved a modicum of fashionable beauty, but she had led a boyish life, hunting and fishing with her brother, and so she had acquired only a very few social graces.

Richard, on the other hand, was large and broad-shouldered. He had thick brown hair and hazel eyes set in a pleasant tanned face. His expression was usually open and cheerful.

The brandy coiled its way down the depths of Amanda's empty stomach. The fire crackled cheerfully on the hearth. Amanda hitched a fire screen in front of her and slid the embroidered oval down the pole to shield her face from the blaze.

"You remember how we used to read the tales of Robin Hood?" she asked dreamily, leaning her head against one wing of the chair and resting the brandy glass on her small stomach.

"Yes," said Richard. "Capital they were. Taking to a life of crime, Amanda?"

"It's worth thinking about," said Amanda, still in the same dreamy voice. "The landlord at the Feathers at Hember Cross told me one day that highwaymen do not just hold up a coach at random. They ferret out news about who is likely to be travelling and when. Some of the ostlers are in their pay."

"*Not* the ostlers at the Feathers," said Richard, leaning forward to pour himself another glass. He held out the bottle to Amanda, who lazily raised her glass to show that she still had some.

"There is this assembly on Friday at the Feathers. We are invited, of course. If we pawned something, Richard, and bought some finery, we could go."

"Now, why should we go?" Richard grinned. "Do you hope to catch a rich beau? As I pointed out earlier, it's not as if you were—"

"Yes, yes, *yes*," said Amanda crossly. "I was thinking we might take to the High Toby."

Richard sat up so abruptly that some of his brandy spilled on his breeches.

"Become highwaymen!" he gasped.

"Why not?" asked Amanda, being made calm and falsely reasonable by brandy on an empty stomach. "The thief-takers are only expert in finding people of the criminal class. No one will think of us. The Earl of Hardforshire's house party is to attend the assembly, and there are a great deal of swells among them. All we have to do is find out discreetly when they plan to take the road."

Richard shook his head as if to clear it. "But to take the first part of the plan," he said. "What on earth have we got left that we could possibly take to the two-to-one shop?"

"The gold locket Mother left me."

"I thought you swore never to part with that."

"No, I did think that, but you see, I would rather eat than not, and one cannot eat a gold locket. Furthermore, the vicar says it is sinful to put too much store by worldly possessions, and a gold locket is a very worldly possession. Also, we shall be like Robin Hood. We are robbing the rich to give to the poor."

"The poor?"

"Us, *stoopid*!"

"It's mad," sighed Richard, "but nonetheless. . . ."

He smiled across at his sister, who smiled back, and despite the dissimilarity of their features, in that brief second they looked amazingly alike.

"Nonetheless," went on Richard slowly, "we do not need to actually *do* it. We could pawn the locket and get the clothes and go to the assembly and just . . . well . . . *see*."

"My idea exactly," said Amanda, putting her feet up on the fender. But in her mind's eye, she and Richard were already out on the King's Highway calling on some bloated lord with more money than was good for his soul to part with some of it.

The next day brought rain, fine drizzling rain, which turned to ice as soon as it hit the ground.

The glorious plans of the night before seemed like a childish fantasy, and without referring to it, Richard and Amanda had each privately decided the whole thing was madness induced by stress and brandy.

But their "uncle's" heir, Mr. Brotherington, chose to pay them a visit. Aunt Matilda was mercifully still asleep.

He was a thick, brutish-looking man with a harsh red face and small black eyes. An expensive morning coat was stretched across his shoulders and his cravat was tied in a travesty of the Oriental, which meant his starched shirt points were cutting into his jowls. He wore an old-fashioned wig and smelled of sweat, imperfectly disguised by musk. His lower limbs dropped from the heights of fashion, being encased in moleskin breeches and square-toed boots caked with mud.

It transpired he had had a lecture from the lawyer, a

lecture from the vicar, and a lecture from the local squire over his lack of concern for the destitute Colbys.

And so he had assumed that the Colbys had put these worthy gentlemen up to it and had come to give them a piece of his mind.

The Colby twins bristled with rage but were not in the way of contradicting their elders. At last, Mr. Brotherington, having had his say uninterrupted, allowed his coarse features to relax in the semblance of a smile and said he had found work for Amanda which would enable her to take up her rightful role in life.

"Which is?" demanded Amanda, her normally pale face flushed.

"As companion to my daughter, Priscilla."

Amanda looked at Richard and shook her head in a disbelieving sort of way. Priscilla, although only two years older than Amanda, was spoiled and overbearing and had inherited the worst of her father's bullying qualities.

"I would rather *starve,*" she said passionately.

"Then starve," said Mr. Brotheringron viciously. "You Colbys were always too top-lofty in your ways. Nothing like a few hunger pangs to bring the pair of you down a peg. You've done nothing but set yourself apart and look down your noses at my Priscilla. Well, you'll get your comeuppance. I'll tell Squire how you sneered at the very idea of genteel work, Amanda Colby."

"*Miss* Amanda to you, Mr. Brotherington," said Amanda sweetly. She went and held open the door. "*And* may I remind you, sir, since you so clumsily aspire to rise in the ranks of the beau-monde, that a *gentleman* making a call never stays above ten minutes, and you have been prosing on for quite twenty."

"Pah!" shouted Mr. Brotherington, cramming his hat down on his wig.

Richard took a step forward and loomed over him.

Mr. Brotherington cast him a fulminating look and strode from the room.

Amanda whirled about and ran upstairs, her old-fashioned chintz skirts flying about her slippers. In two minutes she was back, the gold locket clutched in one hand.

"Take it to the pawn," she said to Richard.

Richard slowly held out his hand, a troubled look on his face.

"What ails you, Richard?" demanded Amanda sharply. "I would rather die of hempen fever than die of poverty."

"Don't talk cant," said Richard automatically. "If you mean you would rather hang, then say so."

"Then what is the matter?" asked Amanda. "You are not worrying about your own neck, I trust?"

"Not I," said Richard. "It is just . . . I am afraid—"

"A Colby *afraid*!"

"Let me finish. I am afraid I cannot dance, so how can I escort you to the assembly?"

"Oh, Richard," laughed Amanda. "The vicar's wife, you know, Mrs. Jolly, taught me *all* the steps. I shall teach you. Now, *go* before Aunt wakes up. She must not know our plans."

But rage, like Dutch courage induced by brandy, did not fuel the Colbys for very long. Again, each privately put aside their rosy dreams of highwaymen. But they had taken a large step in deciding to attend the assembly. Even Richard confessed to a feeling of excitement. Aunt Matilda was roused from her stupor and firmly told that she must act as chaperone to Amanda, Richard succeeding in almost convincing his dithering, trembling aunt that a refurbished Amanda might catch the eye of some wealthy gentleman. Aunt Matilda eagerly seized the fantasy as a way of escaping from the very real problems of incipient poverty and agreed to make Amanda's gown. She was an expert dressmaker and a very quick worker, provided her interest could be kept on the task long enough.

The news of the Colbys' poverty had spread like wildfire throughout the county. The pawnbroker, Mr. Benjamin, gave Richard a handsome sum for the gold locket.

Mr. Johnston, who ran the haberdashery and grocery shop combined, insisted that a bale of sea-green silk was damaged in one corner and would accept only a trifling sum for it. The tailor, Mr. Easterman, presented Richard with a fine suit of evening clothes, explaining they had been ordered by a gentleman of Richard's size some months ago who had failed to collect them. He refused immediate payment, suggesting Richard should supply him with a small monthly sum instead.

The difficulty of getting to the assembly was solved by the vicar, Mr. Jolly, and his wife, who explained they could not attend, as their children were all suffering from a bout of chickenpox, but that they would send their John on the important night with the vicarage carriage to convey the Colbys to the ball.

"It was all very successful," explained Richard as he returned on foot from Hember Cross with his purchases piled up on a handcart. "We should have done this before, Amanda. People are amazingly kind."

He spread out the bale of silk. "See what Mr. Johnston gave me? You will look very fine, Amanda."

"She cannot wear that!" exclaimed Aunt Matilda, holding up her mittened hands in terror. "Young girls must wear white, or at least a pastel color."

"Well, that's dashed ungrateful of you," said Richard hotly. Then he recalled that Aunt Matilda thought the finery was to be paid out of the monthly allowance, and added quickly, "If I had paid a regular price, Aunt, then we could not have *lived* for another month. And Easterman, the tailor, has given me a fine suit of clothes and says I need to pay him only a little a month, and by next month anyway I will have found work."

"A Colby *work*!" Aunt Matilda burst into tears while the twins looked at her in exasperation.

How hard it was, thought Amanda, to feel sympathy for someone in tears who always seemed to *be* in tears. But she put a coaxing arm about her aunt's waist and said, "You forget, Aunt Matilda, that if you manage to make me look very fine, then I might catch the attention of some kind gentleman, and then all your troubles will be over. And with my unfortunate color of hair, I would look quite terrible in pastels. There is no need to nod your head *quite* so vigorously, Richard! You might make a push to pretend I am attractive to the opposite sex instead of making me feel Friday-faced every time you look at me."

More coaxing, more pleading, and several rallying cups of tea were needed to remove the specter of work from Aunt Matilda's mind.

"She really is an amazingly dim-witted woman," said Amanda with all the intolerance of youth, once Aunt

Matilda was at last safely engaged in cutting out material. "Do you think, Richard, that if one cries and cries, one's brain cells become damp and do not function as well as they ought?"

"Never mind that," said Richard, walking through the door at the back of the hall and out onto the shaggy grass of the lawn. "I've been thinking. There is nothing up with work, Amanda. It seems downright immoral to take someone's money away from him by robbery."

And Amanda, who had been thinking that very same thought, suddenly felt cross and argumentative.

"I don't see anything so very bad in taking a few jewels and trinkets away from people who would not miss them," she protested.

"Just imagine if everyone felt like that," replied Richard. "There would be a terrible revolution, like the one in France."

"But we are only thinking of doing it *once*. . . ."

"Have you thought how I am to get *rid* of these baubles? I don't know any fencing kens."

"What has a fencing academy got to do with—?"

"A fence is a receiver of stolen goods. Usually a low type of pawnbroker."

"Oh," said Amanda, breaking off a shrivelled rose head. The day was a sad sort of uniform gray. The morning's hoarfrost was only melting in the center of the lawn but still glittered whitely in the uncut shaggy grass at the verges. A starling perched on the edge of a branch and sent down one long, dismal, piping note. Woodsmoke drifted lazily across the fields from someone's bonfire, carried by the lightest of breeze.

"Oh," said Amanda again in a dismal note like that of the starling. Then her face brightened. "But we could travel to London, Richard, and find one of these low places. We could tell, you know, by simply *looking* at the pawnbroker. The marks of his evil life would be writ on his features. Or rather, that's what they say in the sort of books I read."

"We'll see." Richard shrugged, fighting down a rosy dream of venturing down noisome London alleys with only his father's rusty sword as protection. "At least we are taking some sort of action. We may as well go to this ball. Perhaps some grand person might like to employ me as a secretary."

Amanda giggled. "Not unless he doesn't want to read his own letters. Your writing is atrocious."

"Then I shall run away to sea," said Richard cheerfully. "You can dress in boy's clothes and come along as a cabin boy and we'll sail to South America and find gold."

"And I shall come back a fine lady," sang Amanda, dancing across the lawn.

Richard laughed, running after her. "There's work to be done, I have logs to chop and you have all those berries to turn into jam."

He put an arm around her waist, and, laughing together, they went into the house.

They had had a long childhood, unmarred by any of the doubts and fears of adolescence. Amanda's dreams of love and marriage were still those of a schoolgirl.

The twins were about to be forced to grow up.

2

Friday seemed quite far away one moment and then it was upon them. Aunt Matilda was the calmest of the three, the smell of hot hair from the curling tongs, the smells of scent and new silk and pomade reminding her of the days of her youth.

Her busy needle had transformed the sea-green silk into a demure ball gown with puffled sleeves and deep flounces at the hem. She had bravely sacrificed one of her old silk gowns to trim the hem with a thin border of gold silk and to make Amanda a handsome gold silk stole. Amanda had a pair of white kid gloves, although the palms were somewhat soiled. At last it was decided they would have to do and Amanda must remember never to show the palms of her gloves.

Amanda's hair had been curled and brushed out and curled again, and each time it fought its way back into a soft aureole of auburn frizz.

It was decided to leave it as it was and decorate it with a pretty crown of ivy leaves, fashioned by Richard. He threaded the leaves with a gold watch chain and ornamented the base of each leaf with a

THE VISCOUNT'S REVENGE 25

small pearl taken from a box of loose ones found in the attic.

Richard himself looked magnificent, thought Amanda proudly. His face was lightly tanned and his thick dark brown hair had been curled and pomaded in what they all hoped was the latest of styles. His coat was a little tight across the shoulders but the knee breeches fitted his legs to perfection, and although one of his white silk stockings had an irremovable stain, it was on the inside of one leg and Amanda said if he danced only the very *fast* dances, no one would notice.

Aunt Matilda stunned them both by transforming herself into a stately dowager in a gown of crimson velvet made from the sitting-room curtains, with a huge crimson velvet turban decorated with gold fringe from the sofa in the morning room.

Amanda herself was looking remarkably pretty. The wreath in her auburn hair, the flush of animation in her thin face, and the green of her gown, which brought out the green in her hazel eyes, made her look like a wood nymph.

But Richard only saw his sister looking much as she always did and complimented her with such false heartiness that Amanda began to feel insecure about her appearance. She was just wondering whether her coronet of ivy leaves would be damned as *farouche* and was debating whether to remove it, when the vicarage carriage arrived, and in the bustle of departure, she forget about everything else but the heady excitement of going to her first ball.

They did not speak on the journey into Hember Cross. Richard was trying to memorize dance steps and kept cautiously shuffling his feet and humming under his breath. Amanda was wondering if perhaps *he* would be there, that tall, handsome man who would miraculously supply her with money, security, children, a home, and love—in that order.

The carriage began to rattle over the cobbles of the streets of Hember Cross.

In the houses on either side, winking candles could be seen descending from the upper rooms as the young ladies of the market town made their way downstairs to wait for their carriages. Some people were heading for the Feathers on foot, a link boy bobbing in front of them through the cold blackness of the autumn night.

By the time they approached the street leading to the Feathers, they had to crawl forward in line behind other carriages and gigs, flies and chaises and traps.

Amanda was all for walking, but Aunt Matilda had put on the airs of a dowager with her new gown and said languidly that it would not be at all the thing.

And then, just as the entrance to the inn was in sight, all the vehicles had to pull over to the side of the road while three splendid carriages bowled past. The Earl of Hardforshire's party must be given preference.

"I think it is very uncivil of him," said Amanda crossly, and Aunt Matilda gave a patronising titter and sighed. "The ways of the world, my dear. The ways of the world."

By the time they were able to alight in the inn courtyard, an hour had passed, and Amanda felt cold and cross. They were badly jostled by the press of people in the narrow entrance to the inn. One dumpy girl trod on Amanda's foot, glared at her, and said, "What on earth are *you* doing here?"

Priscilla Brotherington in pastel pink, and looking as

nasty as her father, thought Amanda viciously. She smiled sweetly at Priscilla and kicked her in the ankle.

Richard edged Amanda forward through the press. Aunt Matilda and Amanda went off to leave their cloaks and Richard stood in the anteroom waiting for them, his eyes going over the dress of the other guests.

Familiar faces seemed to spring out of the crowd, and he began to relax. His evening suit was every bit as good as, if not better than, the dress of the young men who surrounded him. The girls, he observed, were very pretty and all wore white or pastel colors. It was not fashionable for young unmarried girls to wear much more in the way of jewellery than a string of pearls, a locket, or a necklace of coral, so he surmised that Amanda's lack of jewellery would go unnoticed.

But he did wish he had refused the sea-green silk. None of the other girls was wearing anything like it.

He felt uneasy as Amanda appeared on Aunt Matilda's arm. His sister did not look at all like the other girls, thought Richard. It must be that gown and that curst wreath in her hair, he reflected miserably, forcing a smile on his face as he stepped forward to escort the two ladies into the ballroom.

Couples were prancing their way noisily through a country dance when the Colby party entered, blinking in the sudden blaze from hundreds of candles. The master of ceremonies, Mr. Jessamyn, who was also the hunt secretary, was loudly calling the figures of the dance from a dais at the end of the room.

Richard seated Aunt Matilda and Amanda on two of the little gilt chairs which lined one wall of the assembly room and went off to fetch them lemonade.

The tinny band struck the last chord and the ladies sank into low curtsies before their bowing partners.

"That must be the earl and his party," said Aunt Matilda, waving towards the fireplace on the other side of the room where a richly dressed group of people was standing.

Amanda looked, and stared. She knew the earl and the countess by sight, but it was the splendour of their guests' attire that first riveted her attention. Never before had she seen so many jewels. They blazed on men and women alike: diamonds, rubies, sapphires, and the inevitable fashionable garnets, winking in the light from the flames of the fire behind them. Two of the younger women wore muslin gowns so thin and transparent that little was left to the imagination. The blonde one had damped her gown so that it clung to every curve. Her dark-haired companion had not, but the material of her gown and petticoat was almost transparent and Amanda was amazed to see that she wore jewels on her garters. Obviously neither of the young ladies had been told by their parents that unmarried girls should wear only simple jewellery.

The women caught her wide-eyed stare and glared haughtily back and then turned and said something to a very tall man who was standing with his back to the room.

He pivoted around and lifted his quizzing glass and gazed full and insolently at Amanda, who quickly raised her fan to cover her face.

When she finally found the courage to peep over her fan, he had turned his attention to the blonde lady in the clinging gown.

Amanda drew a long breath. He was like a hero from one of the gothic novels she avidly read on wet afternoons.

He had a very handsome, bad-tempered face, and every reader of romantic novels knew the hero must be smouldering and angry.

He had very thick hair worn longer than the current fashion. His gaze was steady and watchful under heavy lids. His face was strong and handsome—or rather it would have been handsome had not his mouth been compressed into such a grim line.

He had a high-bridged nose. His eyes were a pale colour, or rather they appeared to have no colour at all. He was tailored to perfection in a blue evening coat and the long skin-fitting trousers made popular by Mr. Brummell, that leader of London fashion. His sculptured cravat rose above a silk waistcoat embroidered with silver thread.

He turned his head slightly and looked full at Amanda again, who immediately blushed, feeling she had been caught out gawking like a yokel.

Richard came back carrying two glasses of lemonade. "I say, Amanda," he said nervously. "The next dance is a Scotch reel and I think I remember it quite well. Perhaps you had better partner me. I wouldn't want to fall over some unfortunate female's feet."

"Well, don't fall over mine," said Amanda tartly.

Considering Amanda had only ever danced with the vicar's wife and Richard had only recently learned to dance with Amanda, they performed very well, both being endowed with a natural grace.

And since they were both still very much children, they left the floor very pleased with themselves and quite prepared to dance with anyone in the room.

After that, Amanda danced with most of the young men of the county and Richard with all the prettiest girls.

But Richard also found time to make several trips to the refreshment room, and before he realised just how much he had drunk, he had accepted a bet from his friend Tommy Potter to go and ask one of the ladies in the earl's party to dance

Now, it had been marked that none of the earl's party had taken the floor. They seemed content to stare at the dancers in a haughty, amused kind of way and then turn and talk among themselves.

Flushed with wine and the thought that Tommy would have to fork out ten guineas if he were successful, Richard marched towards the earl's group, bowed low before the dark-haired lady in the diaphanous muslin gown, and asked for the honour of the next dance.

The lady was the Honourable Cecily Devine, who had been trying to charm her companion, Viscount Charles Hawksborough, to no avail. She raked Richard up and down with a haughty assessing glance which took in his open friendly expression, the breadth of his shoulders, and the strength of his legs.

Amanda, watching breathlessly from the other end of the room, thought it was almost as if the lady were about to take out a stick and poke Richard like a prize pig.

Then Miss Devine shrugged a bare shoulder. "I do not dance," she said wearily.

Lord Hawksborough, the tall, black-haired man who had stared at Amanda, now turned his cold gaze on Miss Devine. "You have been pleading with me for quite an hour to dance," he said in a light, mocking voice. "I do not like contrary women."

"Oh, but you must understand—" began Miss Devine.

"My name is Hawksborough," said the viscount, according Richard a half-bow. "Your partner is Miss Devine." And with that he turned his back on them.

"Oh, well," said Miss Devine, "if I must, I must." She gave rather a shrill laugh and allowed Richard to lead her into a set which was being made up for yet another country dance.

Miss Devine was feeling petulant and angry. She had been invited to the earl's dreadful house party to be a partner to the viscount and he had eluded her at every turn. He had spent most of his time out riding or shooting or fishing. And her hostess, Lady Hardforshire, had gone so far as to imply her clothes were *fast*. But up until a few moments ago, the evening had been fun.

She had enjoyed standing with the viscount beside the fire, noticing out of the corner of her long blue eyes the shocked glances of the countryfolk as they rested on her dress. She had enjoyed their consternation when it dawned on these yokels that not one of the earl's party was going to favour one of them with a dance. And now Lord Hawksborough had *forced* her to dance with this youth. But he was handsome and quite enchanting, she decided, noticing the warm admiration in Richard's eyes as they waited for the music to begin.

She was beginning to mellow when her mouth fell open with surprise and she pushed it shut with the handle of her fan.

Lord Hawksborough was leading that peculiar little girl who had stared at him so much into the dance.

How *dare* he? thought Miss Devine savagely. And at

that moment she saw Richard smiling at a group of youths who were *winking* and leering at him from the side of the floor. It was merely Richard's good-natured friends, including Tommy, congratulating him on his success, but for the haughty Miss Devine, it was enough. She decided to pretend to sprain her ankle during the first steps of the dance.

Accordingly, as soon as she danced across the set to join Richard, she stumbled artistically. But the floor had been enthusiastically covered in a whole snowstorm of French chalk by the village boys before the dance, and it was slippier than it had ever been before. So instead of subsiding artistically, one foot skidded out from under her and she landed up at Richard's feet, banging into his legs.

He bent to pick her up, but she struggled furiously away from him, and in an effort to reach forward and help her, he overbalanced and slipped on the treacherous floor and landed full on top of her.

"I am so sorry," said Richard, struggling to his feet, red with embarrassment. Amanda, who had just joined hands across with Lord Hawksborough in a neighbouring set, stopped suddenly and stared in consternation at her brother. Lord Hawksborough tugged impatiently at her hands, but Amanda refused to move.

"You oaf!" screamed Miss Devine. "You great clumsy yokel!" She turned her eyes languishingly in Lord Hawksborough's direction. "Take me away from these peasants," she cried.

Amanda tore her hands from Lord Hawksborough's and rushed to her brother's defense.

"You slipped *deliberately*," said Amanda roundly. "You, madam, are the peasant. Come, Richard!"

"You forget," said the cool voice of Lord Hawksborough at her elbow, "that this dance is promised to me."

Amanda looked around wildly. The music had stopped, the dancers had stopped. Miss Devine was on her feet and her mouth was opening, and Amanda felt sure some really terrible words were about to come out of it. "Darling Richard," said Amanda hurriedly, "Aunt Matilda wishes some refreshment. And we are spoiling the dance."

She turned to Lord Hawksborough and held out her hands. "Forgive me, sir," she said sweetly.

The music struck up again. Richard turned on his heel and strode off smartly in the direction of the refreshment room, his face flaming. Miss Devine rejoined her companions at the fire.

Lord Hawksborough automatically went through the motions of the dance, his mind busy with angry thoughts.

He wished he had never come. The visit had been a disaster and the earl's miserly table a disgrace. There had been bad shooting and worse fishing. The company had been spiteful and dull.

He had only accepted the invitation because he was to escort his sister and mother to London from nearby Bellingham, where his sister had been attending a seminary for young ladies. He had not wanted to dance but had felt obliged to when Miss Devine had forcibly brought it to his attention that the behaviour of the earl's company was uncivil to say the least. And so he had asked this strange little girl who looked so like a fairy princess to dance. But his fairy already had her country lover if that "Darling Richard" was anything to go by. If the earl wished to patronise the country people, let

him do it on his own in future! The viscount was prey
to a violent fit of indigestion, an unromantic complaint
which made him look increasingly brooding and sinister.

Amanda found herself becoming disappointed in him
and also a little bit afraid of him. He was not at all
romantic, she decided. She did not like his eyes. They
were very pale, like pale silver, and he had rather a
fixed look.

Lord Hawksborough performed his part of the country dance with grace, despite a feeling that a greal lump
of burning-hot lava was lodged somewhere under his
cravat. He could never remember having felt so spleenish
before. But then, he could never remember having
eaten such terrible food or drunk such bad wine as he
had at the Earl of Hardforshire's home before.

Supper was announced immediately after the dance,
and he gave a silent groan. He did not want to eat. He
did not want to fight among the jams and jellies in the
next room. He wanted to go home and take rhubarb
pills and forget that such a place as Hember Cross ever
existed.

The guests were already jostling and pushing into
the refreshment room. With a sort of weary courtesy,
he held out his arm to Amanda.

"I can find Richard to take care of me, if you would
rather not," said Amanda.

Lord Hawksborough turned and looked hopefully
about. "Since your Richard is not in sight," he said
with a sigh, "I cannot very well abandon you."

Amanda longed for the courage to say she did not
want to be escorted by any gentleman so obviously
reluctant to do so, but his weary hauteur, his grand
manner, and his great height intimidated her and so

she shyly put a hand on his arm and allowed him to lead her to the supper room.

Lord Hawksborough found them two empty seats at the end of a long table, and half-closed his eyes against the repulsive sight of so much food and drink being piled haphazardly on so many plates. One large young lady in pink had actually helped herself to meat and jelly and cream all at the same time.

He filled a plate with cold meat and vegetables and handed it to Amanda. He poured himself a glass of wine and shook his head when Amanda asked him timidly if he was not going to have anything to eat.

Voices rose and fell about them. The earl, the countess, and their other guests were absent.

Lord Hawksborough looked down at the diminutive figure of his companion and wondered how she managed to stay so slim. She was eating food at an enormous rate.

He tapped his quizzing glass against his empty plate and said, "What do you do for amusement, Miss . . . er . . . ?"

"Colby," said Amanda, glad her mouth was momentarily empty. "Miss Amanda Colby."

"I am Hawksborough. What do you do to pass your country days, apart from attend assemblies?"

"Well, my . . . my lord," began Amanda tentatively, looking quickly up at him from under her lashes. She assumed he had a title. It was very awkward when people gave just one name, but it usually meant they held a peerage. "Well, I do quite a lot at home," she went on candidly. "You know, the washing and making jams and jellies and baking and distilling medicines, and cooking dinner, and weeding the vegetable garden and . . ." She broke off and bit her lower lip in confusion. It all sounded very unexciting.

She had rolled back her gloves to eat and also to hide the soiled palms. Lord Hawksborough noticed her work-reddened hands.

"What energy!" he remarked. "Have you no servants?"

"Oh, yes. A woman from the town cleans a little and a man helps with the garden."

"And you do the rest?"

"Not alone. Aunt Matilda helps, and Richard, of course."

This Richard must be her fiancé, thought the viscount, and yet she wore no ring.

He noticed that she had cocked her head a little on one side while her gold-and-green eyes kept sliding to the other side of the room where the boy called Richard was staring moodily at his food.

Amanda took a deep breath. "May I have some more, my lord?"

"To eat? You have a tremendous appetite."

"I have had nothing since breakfast."

He took her plate and piled it up again, and refilled his glass. The wine was remarkably good and Lord Hawksborough felt himself beginning to relax. He was amused by the quick sharp gestures of this strange girl. She looked like some wild animal poking its head out of its lair to reconnoitre the surrounding countryside.

He suddenly wished she would look full at him. He was not used to being ignored by ladies of any age.

"Then housework is your only amusement?" he pursued.

Amanda carefully chewed and swallowed her food before replying. "I read a great deal," she said. "On wet days, that is. Sometimes I take out the gun and go shooting with Richard."

"An odd pastime for a lady."

"Not if you need something for dinner," said Amanda, beginning to eat again and failing therefore to notice the startled look on his face.

Lord Hawksborough was surprised by Miss Colby's honesty. Most ladies in her penurious position would have pretended to have servants, would have pretended to lead a life of leisure.

A footman placed a large steaming dish of olio almost under his lordship's nose. Chunks of beef, fowl, partridge, and mutton floated in the brown broth. Lord Hawksborough shuddered and raised a scented handkerchief to his nose. Miss Amanda Colby said eagerly, "Oh, do you think I could possibly . . . ?"

"Yes," he said wearily. "You may." But he felt he could not spoon the olio onto her plate and signalled the footman to perform the service for him.

He sat in silence while Amanda demolished her third plateful of food with a hearty appetite. Amanda at last guiltily dabbed her mouth with her napkin and sought in vain for something to say. She felt she should not have eaten so much so quickly. But she had been *ravenous.*

She still felt she had some room left to sample the array of gingerbread and Portugal cakes, ratafia cakes, saffron cakes, ice cream, and jellies. She had never seen so many delicacies before. But what would he think of her?

"If only you would eat something, my lord," she said anxiously.

"So that you may not feel conscience-stricken should you fill your plate again?"

"Exactly, my lord."

"Allow me to assist you. I have not seen such an appetite since Bartholomew Fair."

"I am *not* a freak," said Amanda stiffly.

"Not yet," said his lordship nastily as another twinge of indigestion seized him by the throat.

Amanda's eyes flew up to meet his for the first time. They were amazing eyes, he reflected. Wide and green with glints of gold. They reminded him of a woodland pond in the evening sunlight. They reminded him of spring sunshine flickering on the green of new leaves.

"Forgive me," he said abruptly. "I am impolite because I am a trifle out of sorts." He waved his hand and a footman appeared with a clean plate. He told the footman to fill it with a selection of cakes and pastries.

"Do you perform the waltz at these assemblies?" he asked.

Amanda shook her head. "I think everyone has practised the steps in secret. Even Mrs. Jolly, and she is the vicar's wife. But no one has had the courage to perform publicly, I believe. But I am not very well versed in the social life of the county."

"Odso! Why is that, pray?"

"I have no money."

"Then may I suggest your Richard find work?"

"No, you may not," snapped Amanda. Then she added in a milder tone, "It is a sore point with me, don't you see."

"He could always enter the army," pursued the viscount, noticing idly that her cloud of curly hair glinted faintly with red and gold lights under the stiff, shiny green of her coronet of ivy leaves.

"He cound enter prison, too," said Amanda, wishing he would stop asking questions and allow her a chance to eat just one of the delicious cakes in front of her. "Of what good is the army if one has not a commission? Of what use to be degraded and flogged and beaten?"

"There are quite a number of educated young men serving in the ranks in the Peninsula," he said quietly. "They are not all cannon fodder."

"A fact you know from personal experience, of course?" mocked Amanda, tilting her head a little on one side and studying the elegance of his dress and the whiteness of his long hands.

"As I know from personal experience," he said equably.

"How long do you expect to stay with Lord Hardforshire?" asked Amanda quickly, to change the subject.

"I have finished my stay," he replied, finding himself wishing she would look up at him again, but she addressed all her remarks to those dratted cakes. "I shall stay here tonight, and tomorrow I travel to Bellingham to escort my sister and my mother back to town."

"You will surely not travel by night?" asked Amanda quickly. "I have heard tales of highwaymen . . ."

"And so have I." He smiled. "But not in this county. Lord Hardforshire assures me that highway robbery is unheard of, no doubt because it is a very small county. My mother will very likely wish to travel during the night. She is always anxious to reach London as soon as possible."

"Oh," said Amanda meditatively, her eyes sliding to the magnificent diamond he wore in his cravat.

The viscount fell silent and Amanda seized the opportunity to bite into a cake, while her mind worked furiously. The highwayman idea was only a dream.

What if she and Richard held up Lord Hawksborough! But he looked so tall and imposing, and he *had* been rather pleasant and courteous. Amanda gave a little sigh. How marvellous it would be if you could live inside dreams and never have to face the cold harsh light of reality.

Lord Hawksborough picked up his quizzing glass again and swung it by its cord between his fingers. The light from the chandelier sparked fire from the huge ruby which glowed on his middle finger, held by a thick antique setting of white gold.

Isn't it amazing sad, thought Amanda, that he can calmly talk about Richard finding work when that one ring would probably keep the three of us forever.

Amanda swallowed the remains of her cake and started hurriedly on another. She felt someone watching her across the room and looked over and caught Aunt Matilda's beaming, approving face. Good heavens! Aunt Matilda obviously thought she was fascinating his lordship. That was indeed flying high!

But she *had* been popular this evening, thought Amanda, carefully putting the remains of her cake on the plate. Very. A lot of her partners had been Richard's friends. Richard had lost touch with most of them since he had left school, but he was still regarded as a prime favourite. And they had paid her no end of compliments, so she could not be exactly an antidote.

But she did not know how to flirt, so ran Amanda's busy thoughts. The gentlemen had complimented her on her appearance and on her gown. In the books

Amanda read, the villain always lusted passionately after the heroine, whereas the hero was always hitting his brow and looking on her in a kind of uplifting spiritual way and pressing his lips to her brow. But that was books for you. They were not much help in coping with the here and now. And here and now was one rich and attractive lord. Perhaps he was married.

"Is your wife with you?" asked Amanda suddenly.

"No," he said. "I have no wife."

I must flirt, thought Amanda. At least I could *practise.*

Amanda wrinkled her brow. Then she remembered she had once asked Mrs. Jolly to instruct her in the art of flirting. Mrs. Jolly had said severely that good manners were enough, but had finally relented and said with a smile, "Always keep in mind, Amanda, that the gentlemen like compliments every bit as much as the ladies. I do not think the butter can be spread thick enough!"

What did one say? She had heard one man remark to another at the beginning of the evening, "That gel has a deuced pretty ankle." Perhaps something along those lines. . . .

"You have a very fine leg, my lord," said Amanda.

Lord Hawksborough removed his gaze from the crowded room and fixed her with a pale silver stare. "I do not think I can possibly have heard you aright, Miss Amanda," he said. He glanced down the table and saw a large leg of mutton, and his face cleared. His young companion must have a truly bottomless stomach and the digestion of an ostrich.

"You were requesting some mutton?"

"No," said Amanda, all pretty puzzlement. "I said you have a very fine leg."

"Indeed!" he replied politely.

"Yes," said Amanda earnestly. "I think it is very well shaped."

"I cannot return the compliment," he said gently, "for obvious reasons."

"And . . . and . . ." pursued the resolute Amanda, wishing her brother could hear how gamely she was flirting with this lord, "your eyes are like . . . are like . . ." Her voice faltered as she met his flat silver stare. "Like sixpences," she finished lamely.

"What about my left eyebrow?" he asked.

Amanda studied it carefully. "Arched like Cupid's bow?" she suggested hopefully.

"No, no," he said sadly. "You have failed to please me. A *mouth*, my dear Miss Amanda, is compared to a Cupid's bow. What can one say of an eyebrow? Like a hairy caterpillar's back arched in the sun?"

"No," said Amanda, "I do not think that would do *at all*. I am persuaded you are bamming me."

"When you have praised my leg so beautifully? I can assure you that no female of my acquaintance has ever appreciated my poor leg so much before. When I die, I shall have it embalmed and sent to you."

Amanda gave a snort of laughter. "I was trying to flirt, my lord, because it is the thing to do, don't you see, but obviously I do not know the right way to go about it."

"Then you need lessons." He picked up her hand and held it lightly in his and smiled into her eyes. "I could teach you. . . ."

The sound of a shrill exclamation made him turn around. Amanda followed his gaze.

The earl and countess, Miss Devine, and the other

members of the earl's house party were standing in the doorway with the master of ceremonies, Mr. Jessamyn. Mr. Jessamyn had told the earl in no uncertain terms that the behaviour of his guests had offended most of the county present at the ball. Furthermore, Miss Devine's insults had been too much. The earl had agreed to remove the members of his party forthwith. Mr. Jessamyn as hunt secretary was allowed a license given to few and spoke his mind in the ballroom as he spoke his mind on the hunting field.

Miss Devine was furious that the earl had not stood upon his rank. *She* was not going to stand and shuffle her feet in disgrace and allow herself to be patronised by a set of country nobodies.

"Then *come along*," she said in a loud carrying voice. "I am still feeling shaken after having been jumped on by some great ploughboy."

There was a shocked silence and then everyone started to talk at once. Amanda's eyes flew across the room to where her brother sat. His face was red with mortification.

"Excuse me one moment, my lord," she said breathlessly. "I must go to Richard," and without waiting for his reply she hurried off.

"Oh, Richard," whispered Amanda, sliding into an empty chair beside him. "She is horrible, that woman. Do not look so stricken, I beg of you."

"Damn them," said Richard fiercely. "I would rob the lot if I could."

"Oh, Richard, do not refine too much on it. She is spoilt. She dresses like a Cyprian. Oh, see, they are leaving. I must say good-bye to Lord Hawksborough and then I will return."

As Amanda left to join Richard, Lord Hawksborough

experienced a stab of what he was sure was indigestion as he watched her slight figure move quickly across the room.

He found the earl at his elbow and rose to his feet. "Well, Hawksborough," grunted the earl. "Seems some of my ladies have disgraced us. Better get 'em off, heh!"

"Yes," said the viscount wearily. "I will help see the ladies to the carriages."

Unseen by the viscount, Amanda had come back and was standing behind the earl, within earshot.

"Want to say good-bye to your young lady?" said the earl.

"My . . . Oh, the village maiden," said Lord Hawksborough. He still had that pain in his chest and it was getting worse. The evening had been insipid. Miss Amanda had enlivened it considerably, but he would not see her again and she preferred the company of her country lover, Richard.

"No," he went on with quite dreadful clarity. "I shall be glad to leave. I cannot remember when I last spent a more boring evening."

She was so furious, she did not know whether to scream or cry. To be dismissed contemptuously as a bore. She *hated* Lord Hawksborough. She hated him more than Mr. Brotherington. She hated him more than anyone else in all her young life. Amanda turned on her heel and went back to join Richard.

They both sat in silence until Amanda at last put her small hand over Richard's large one and whispered, "Lord Hawksborough is leaving Bellingham sometime tomorrow. He plans to travel to London at night."

"Indeed!" said Richard Colby savagely. "Now, that, my dear Amanda, is very interesting indeed."

They looked at each other in complete understanding.

Aunt Matilda came drifting up, looking rather wilted. Her large turban had sunk down on her forehead so that her faded blue eyes peered warily out at the world through a curtain of gold fringe.

"Who was that extremely handsome man you were having supper with, Amanda?" she asked.

"Lord Hawksborough."

"Hawksborough!" Two spots of pink began to appear on Aunt Matilda's withered cheeks. "Now, I wonder. I just wonder," she murmured.

"Wonder what, Aunt?" demanded Amanda sharply.

"Oh, nothing," said Aunt Matilda airily.

The dance was starting up in the ballroom again, but Amanda and Richard both declared they would like to go home. Amanda had not been to school, having gleaned all her education from Richard's schoolbooks, and so, unlike her brother, had no friends to confide in. Richard, because he was hurt and humiliated, blamed his friends for egging him on to ask the haughty Miss Devine to dance, and wished only to get back to Fox End and lick his wounds.

Both brother and sister were too miserable on the journey back to notice that Aunt Matilda was in unusually high fettle, humming snatches of dance tunes to herself, and smiling and nodding at no one in particular.

Frost glinted and sparkled on the hedgerows like the diamond in Lord Hawksborough's cravat, and a moon rode high above the countryside, as flat and silver as his lordship's eyes.

It was good to be home at last. The quietness of Fox

End welcomed them with its comforting smells of beeswax, woodsmoke, dry rot, and damp plaster.

Aunt Matilda sat an infuriatingly long time over the tea tray. Richard and Amanda wondered whether she intended to go to bed at all. She had removed her turban and her faded eyes sparkled and her wispy salt-and-pepper hair stood up around her head as she talked about the ladies she had met and the food she had eaten.

At last, to their relief, Aunt Matilda announced she was retiring. First she insisted on carrying the tea things to the kitchen and washing them up, despite the protests of the twins.

Then she fussed about the kitchen, picking things up and putting them down.

Then she went into the back kitchen to prod a spoon into Amanda's bramble jam to make sure it had set. Finally she lit her bed candle and mounted the stairs with a light step, singing softly to herself.

"Well," said Amanda in amazement. "It was certainly worth the expense just to see Aunt so happy and *alive.*"

"We did not spend so much," said Richard. "In fact, I could give you some, Amanda."

"No, keep the money," said Amanda, settling herself down in the winged armchair facing Richard. They always used the morning room once the cold weather had set in. The dining room and drawing room were large and chilly and damp. The study was used as a sort of dump for old game bags and papers and unanswered letters and bills.

Richard sat with his legs stretched out in front of him, thoughtfully watching the leaping flames. Amanda felt a pang of dismay and loss. All at once he looked older and his old carefree expression had gone.

"What are you thinking about?" she asked.

"Money," he said. "Money and how to get it. I will never allow anyone to humiliate me as I was humiliated this evening."

"I was humiliated too," said Amanda in a low voice. She told him of Lord Hawksborough's remark to the earl.

"How dare he!" she went on passionately. "Are we not as good as they? Even the lord lieutenant of the county, Sir Percival Jenks, would not treat us so." A mischievous smile curved her lips and she leaned forward, resting her elbows on her knees in a most unladylike manner. "I say, Richard," she said softly, "would it not be extremely humiliating for my Lord Hawksborough to be held up by two highwaymen, one of them on a donkey?"

Richard grinned back and then his face grew serious. "I had better ride into Bellingham in the morning and find out how many servants they have. It would not be at all funny if they were armed—well, they will be armed of course—what I am trying to say is that it would be disastrous if they should be young, alert servants who would shoot us on sight."

"I think it would be infinitely worse if we shot anyone ourselves."

"I thought of that," said Richard simply, "and I shall not load the pistols."

Amanda looked at her brother thoughtfully. She was glad he did not propose to leave her out of the venture, but on the other hand it would be a *start* if one's brother saw one as a frail female to be defended from the cares of the world.

But instead she asked, "Are the pistols in good condition? I have not used one since you taught me how to shoot two years ago."

"I cleaned and oiled them and refaced the flints," said Richard. The Colbys both knew that in a flintlock pistol, the contact of flint and steel caused the flint to chip away slightly at every shot.

Neglect led to misfires, the average being one misfire for every thirty-eight successful shots. "Not that I'm going to load them, as I said," pointed out Richard, "but there is something very deadly about a well-cleaned, well-oiled pistol."

"Do you think," ventured Amanda cautiously, "that we will wake up tomorrow and find our tempers have cooled and that the whole thing is all rather childish?"

"No," said Richard grimly, "I want revenge."

"Perhaps if I had not spent so much time with the wicked Lord Hawksborough, I might have attracted some other man. Several young gentlemen told me . . . oh, so many flattering things." Amanda sighed.

"That's because I told m'friends to," said Richard heartlessly. "Thought it would put that Priscilla Brotherington's nose out of joint a little."

"Oh," said Amanda in a small voice. Then her face brightened. "But several of them were *not* your friends, Richard, and they said pretty things too."

"Eh?" Richard studied his sister. Her face was tired and wan and her coronet of leaves had curled and drooped. "Better stick to robbery," he said in a kind, brotherly voice.

"Oh," said Amanda dismally. "Did . . . did . . . you meet any pretty girls, Richard?"

"Scores of 'em," he said, looking infuriatingly smug. "There was one girl called Belinda Tring-Carter. She had the neatest figure you ever saw, and lots and lots of glossy, smooth curls . . . like . . . like silk. I danced with her twice. You know, Amanda, I'm glad we went to that assembly. I've realised that it might be jolly to set up house on one's own with a pretty charmer. Also, that wretched Devine female gave me just the courage I need to hold up Hawksborough's coach."

"*She* won't be in it."

"Oh, don't be too sure of that," said Richard. "There was gossip flying about that she and Lord Hawksborough are expected to make a match of it."

"Then they are very well suited," snapped Amanda.

She had a throbbing pain over her right temple and was overcome with a sudden desire to get away from her brother for the first time in her life. He was the only man she had ever been close to, and she thought he might at least have made some push to tell her that she had been successful at the ball. She had sat out only three dances. But Richard would probably take credit for that as well as say he had told all his friends to dance with her.

"I must go to bed," she said, rising wearily to her feet.

"I'll sit here for a bit," said Richard. "I have to make plans. I have to decide the best place to waylay the coach."

"As to that," said Amanda thoughtfully, "I thought the best place would be on Fern Hill. It is very steep and has trees on either side. The coach will be going very slowly, so there is no danger of them charging past, and we will be screened by the trees until they arrive."

There was a little silence and then Richard said, "Just what I had decided on myself."

"No, you didn't," said Amanda in great irritation. "You didn't think of it at all. You only say that so that you can take the credit. You're always doing things like that."

And then, to the dismay of both, she burst into tears and ran from the room and upstairs to bed.

Amanda flung herself on the bed and sobbed her heart out. She had always looked up to Richard, followed him in all his boyish, and then manly, pursuits. Richard always told her what to do. It was Richard who had to teach her to read and write, Richard who had taught her how to shoot and how to fish. But the hard fact that her brother saw her neither as a woman nor as an intelligent girl but merely as some sort of small boy, tagging at his coattails, cut her deeply. Because they were twins and loved one another, Amanda had assumed they thought alike and were of the same character.

But for the first time Richard appeared in her eyes as a rather . . . yes, *callow* young man.

Were all men so? Were they young and clumsy like Richard or old and sneering and bitter like Lord Hawksborough? And he *was* old, thought Amanda, scrubbing her eyes dry with a corner of the sheet. He must be thirty if he was a day. And to think at one point she had thought him attractive!

Now all she wanted to see was the look of fear on his lordship face as he looked down the barrels of the Colbys' pistols.

Her eyes began to close. There was Miss Devine to get even with, of course. But when she and Richard had pawned the stolen jewels and gambled successfully on the stock exchange with the proceeds and had thousands and thousands of pounds, then they could deal with Miss Devine.

Amanda walked off into a dream where she entered a London ballroom wearing a gown made wholly from diamonds, on the arm of a handsome man with *fair* hair and *blue* eyes.

But, in reality, still wearing her green ball gown and with her coronet of ivy crushed into the pillow, Miss Amanda Colby fell fast asleep.

3

The following day was warmer as the wind moved around to the southwest. Great fleecy clouds scudded across a hazy blue sky. The whole countryside seemed in motion. Leaves of gold and brown and red and amber flew before the wind, dancing across the burnt stubble as if dancing on tiptoe, swirling in clouds, up and up, as if trying to reach the heavens, and then swooping down again to continue their headlong dance across the fields.

Amanda slept late and awoke to the sound of a shutter banging somewhere downstairs. She was amazed to find she had slept in her clothes, and stripped off and washed herself from head to foot, standing in a flowered china basin and pouring cold water from two brass-bound cans over her body.

She scrubbed herself down with a huckaback towel until she glowed, and then quickly donned her faded, yellowing underwear and an old gray wool round gown. She pulled a chintz mobcap over her hair and ran downstairs. The house appeared to be empty. Richard would have gone into Bellingham to spy out the land, but there was not even a sense of her aunt's presence. She ran up again and pushed open her aunt's bedroom door. The bed was neatly made, but of her aunt there was no sign.

Perhaps Aunt Matilda, still revived by the excitement of the ball, had walked down to the vicarage to talk to Mrs. Jolly.

Amanda decided to occupy herself with the household chores until Richard or her aunt should return. She went around to the stables at the back of the house, catching her breath as a great buffet of warm wind struck her as she turned a corner of the building. She led Bluebell out of his stall and turned him out into the field at the bottom of the garden.

The field now belonged to Mr. Brotherington but it was not used for anything and surely even he would not object to one small donkey using it for grazing.

Bluebell was rather an ill-favored donkey, being slightly cross-eyed and dusty-coated. He was given to erratic turns of speed but Amanda had become used to this and pointed out to any critic that most donkeys would not budge at all.

She wished she had a good, well-behaved horse to take on a mission like highway robbery. But Bluebell it would have to be. The animal was not without a certain intelligence fuelled by low cunning, and had a passion for sugar loaves.

The whole of the day began to take on an air of unreality. Amanda's mind flinched away from the prospect of the night to come.

She left Bluebell and went into the back kitchen. The jam had to be put into jars and sealed. I could sell this, thought Amanda, for about tenpence a pot. Perhaps I should think along these domestic lines. We cannot possibly be going to hold up a coach!

But in her heart of hearts, she knew that she would, because more than anything else in the world she wanted revenge on Lord Hawksborough.

The jam being finished, Amanda made herself a dish of tea and sat at the kitchen table, looking out vaguely at the trees and bushes in the garden, being shaken and tossed by the blustery wind.

A sudden squall of rain darkened the sky and flung raindrops against the glass of the kitchen window.

New thoughts and frustrations and desires kept springing into Amanda's mind. For the first time, she realised she envied her brother the freedom allowed him by his sex. For the first time she realised that women were destined to have a hard time of it unless they were very lucky. Unless you married a rich man, you were tied body and soul to that jam-and-preserve-making factory called home, and whether you loved your husband or not, childbearing was exacted with a pious and pitiless vigour. Everyone assumed that women had inferior minds.

The wives of the farmers and yeomen of the surrounding countryside automatically adopted their husband's political opinions and never for a moment thought of forming any of their own. They either shopped at a "blue" shop or a "pink" shop, according to their political beliefs. A Tory would consider it very wrong to give custom to a "pink" shopkeeper, and a Whig would avoid a "blue" shop at all costs.

Amanda did not feel that her mind was inferior to Richard's. Despite the fact that she had had no schooling, she knew she had managed to surpass him in knowledge by studying at home every book she could get her hands on. And yet, she wondered, surely the well-balanced, intelligent woman she liked to think herself could have foreseen that Uncle would not live forever. They could have scraped a little each month from the allowance and could have bought a piece of land. The garden at Fox End was laid out like a gentleman's garden in miniature. They did not even keep geese or hens, and the vegetable garden was ridiculously small.

She wondered all at once where Aunt Matilda had gone.

The rain had stopped. She put down her teacup and was just getting ready to attack the rest of the housework when there came a furious banging at the garden door.

A servant Amanda had not seen before stood outside. He was wearing buckskin breeches, white swanskin lapelled waistcoat, and a light-colored cloth cape-coat. Despite his smart dress, his face was coarse and red, with tufts of hair sprouting from his nose and ears.

"That donkey belong 'ere?" he demanded. "Well, you tell your master, my girl, that Mr. Brotherington will shoot that hanimal if 'e finds it on 'is land agin."

Amanda looked at him in trepidation. She could see he obviously mistook her for a servant. She was still wearing her mobcap and had tied an old gingham apron over her dress.

"I brung 'im back in your garding," went on the man, "an' that's where 'e's got to stay, see?"

"Yes, I see," said Amanda faintly.

The man touched his hat and slouched off.

Amanda went back into the kitchen and sat down, vaguely surprised to find her legs were trembling. Why hadn't she sent him to the rightabout?

"Because you were afraid," sneered her inner voice. "Fine upstanding superior woman *you* are. Can't do anything without a man to protect you."

Amanda realised this was only the start of Mr. Brotherington's petty persecutions. He meant to hound them out of Fox End and probably out of the county as well.

She began to clean and dust and polish, working harder than she had ever worked before in order to keep her frightened, jumbled thoughts at bay.

By the time the shadows began to lengthen, Amanda was fast asleep, her head on the kitchen table.

"Well, here's a fine sight!" her brother's voice roused her. "You've been snoring your head off while I do all the work!"

"I've done nothing but work all day," said Amanda furiously. "Do you think this house cleans itself?"

"Oh, *women's* work." Richard shrugged. "Never mind. Everything is set. Nine o'clock's the time we catch 'em."

"What time is it now?" asked Amanda, getting up and lighting a tallow candle at the kitchen fire.

"After six."

"Then we *are* going to do it?"

"Of course," said Richard scornfully. "What's come over you, Amanda? You've gone all soft and sort of trembly, like a girl."

"Well, I *am* a girl. How did you find out?"

"It was easy." Richard grinned. "I thought I would have to disguise myself and go to the seminary and try to bribe one of the servants, but that was not the way it happened. I found the seminary easily enough, and I was wandering around outside, wondering what to do, when this note dropped at my feet. It asked me to go around the back of the school to the garden gate. So I went around—"

"Go on," said Amanda, her eyes glowing with excitement and her fears forgotten.

"Don't interrupt. I went around, and there's this minx of a girl waiting by the garden gate. She had one of those saucy sort of faces, you know, all pink cheeks and big black eyes. She grabbed hold of my arm in such a familiar way and drew me into the garden and handed me a shilling and told me to get her a half-pound of chocolate drops. 'I would *die* for chocolate drops,' she said. She said the food was awful and they were not allowed sweets except on holidays. So I saw my chance and said I would get them and pay for them myself. I would get her a whole pound of chocolate drops, if she would get me a little bit of information and swear never to tell a soul she had seen me. She promised and crossed her heart, so I asked when young Lady Hawksborough would be travelling to London. She looked puzzled and then she said, 'Oh, you mean Susan Fitzgerald.' Hawksborough was made a viscount for some public service or another, but of course his sister and mother still carry the family name.

"Anyway, she said she would tell me after I got the chocolate drops. Which I did.

"Do you know, Amanda, I thought every confectioner's in Bellingham had conspired against me *not* to have chocolate drops?

"But at last I found them and hurried back, praying she'd still be waiting for me. At first I thought she had gone, but then she leapt out from behind a bush, crying, 'Did you get them?'

"I handed over the sweets and asked her for the information. She said she would not give it to me unless I . . . er . . . gave her a kiss," said Richard, turning a dull red. "I did, and she told me that they are to leave at eight o'clock, which means they will reach Fern Hill around nine. You had better wear that old suit of boy's clothes of mine. Good thing we kept them. And we had better wear masks."

"And what was it like?" asked Amanda.

"What like?"

"Kissing Miss Thing."

"Oh, *girls*," said Richard. But he blushed again.

"Did she tell you her name?"

"No," said Richard. "I won't see her again, so what's the point? Do keep your mind on the job, Amanda. We must start getting ready now. Where's Aunt Matilda?"

"I don't know," replied Amanda. "Has she not come back? 'Tis most strange. She has been absent all day."

"Probably gone for her yearly outing," said Richard callously. "Do not worry. She'll come home and go into either strong hysterics or hibernation, one or t'other. Let's hope she does not arrive just as we are leaving, all booted and masked."

It took them quite a time to get ready. Richard insisted they wear the old wool wigs they had worn at Christmas when they were much younger and had staged a play to amuse Aunt Matilda. They were both bright red and made from dyed coarse wool. Richard donned a drab benjamin and lent Amanda his game coat, which came nearly down to her ankles. They put old-fashioned tricornes on their heads and their masks in their pockets and at last they were ready to take the road.

The night was cold and full of the sound of the wind. It had shifted from the south to the east and Amanda shivered with cold and excitement.

Fern Hill was only a short way from where they lived. Bluebell had put on one of his erratic bursts of speed and so they were there well before time, standing in the black shelter of the tossing trees. A little moon rushed high above, in and out of masses of ragged black cloud. Some wild animal crackled in the undergrowth and Amanda nearly fell off her donkey in fright. Her tension mounted as the minutes dragged past, her heart thudding against her ribs. Her mouth felt dry.

Would they never come?

Bluebell shifted restlessly under her. Amanda, near to tears, opened her mouth to say that she wanted to go home and forget about the whole thing, when all of a sudden the lights of the carriage bobbed like fireflies at the bottom of the long slope of Fern Hill.

"This is it!" whispered Richard.

They donned their masks and pulled out their pistols.

The noise of the wind rushing in the trees was so loud that at first they could not hear the sound of the approaching coach. All they could do was watch the twin carriage lights coming closer and closer.

They couldn't . . . they mustn't . . . Dear God . . . *No*! So rushed Amanda's terrified thoughts like the wind rushing in the branches above her head.

And then the carriage was almost upon them.

Richard urged his mount forward. He made a huge, black, menacing figure.

"Stand and deliver!" he yelled in a great voice.

The coachman on the box pulled on the reins and slewed the coach around sideways so that it would not slide back down the steep incline. He reached under his box.

"Raise your hands," yelled Richard, "or I'll send you to your Maker!"

The coachman raised his hands. The groom next to him did the same.

"And you on the back," shouted Richard. "Round in front with your hands above your heads."

Two footmen emerged from the rumble at the back. Richard thanked God there were no outriders.

"Keep them covered," he called to Amanda.

He dismounted and strode to the door of the coach and wrenched it open.

"Outside," he barked.

Lord Hawksborough's face was such a mask of cold fury that Richard's pistol trembled for a moment in his hand. An elderly lady with Lord Hawksborough's peculiar colorless eyes was helped down by a plain, severe-looking girl in a poke bonnet—Lord Hawksborough's mother and sister. Richard held out a sack. He held the pistol straight at Lord Hawksborough's mother and snarled, "Drop your jewels in there or I'll shoot the old girl."

"Do as he says," said Lord Hawksborough bitterly.

He was cursing the fact that his mother had insisted they travel in her old cumbersome travelling coach with only her aged servants as guard.

"There's someone else in there!" said Richard, hearing a sound from the carriage. "Out!"

A trembling maid appeared, tears rolling down her face. "I tried to guard your jewel box, ma'am," she whimpered to Lord Hawksborough's mother, Mrs. Fitzgerald.

"Now we *all* know about the jewels," said Lord Hawksborough wearily. "You may as well hand them over."

Sobbing, the maid put the jewel box in Richard's capacious sack.

"I hope that satisfies your greed," said his lordship acidly.

"You have forgotten something," said Richard, keeping his voice gruff.

Amanda, watching and listening, prayed Richard would finish and get them away, as far away as possible.

"What is that?" she heard Lord Hawksborough's icy voice asking.

"Your ring, my lord."

Oh, no, thought Amanda, white to the lips.

Slowly Lord Hawksborough drew off the ring. His eyes were like diamond chips as he stared at Richard, and Richard felt a cold shiver of fear run through him.

"I will find you, if it takes my life and my fortune," said his lordship in pleasant, even tones which were more terrifying than if he had ranted and raved. "I will find you," he repeated, "and you will hang. You will not escape me."

"Back in the coach," growled Richard. "The old lady last."

Lord Hawksborough gave Richard one long measuring look and helped his sister into the coach. Mrs. Fitzgerald turned and followed them and slammed the door behind her. Neither she nor her daughter had uttered a word.

Richard rode back to Amanda.

"Move on!" he yelled to the coachman.

The coachman picked up the reins and cracked his whip. The coach surged forward.

"*Move,*" hissed Richard to Amanda.

He spurred his mount and was off through the trees. Amanda drove her heels into Bluebell's fat sides, but the animal refused to budge.

Suddenly a bullet whistled through Amanda's hat and Bluebell jumped violently and set off headlong through the trees. Lord Hawksborough had climbed through the carriage window opposite from the side of the road Richard had been on, had climbed on the box and seized the coachman's horse pistol and had fired straight at Amanda. The terrified coachman, trying to help, had only succeeding in hindering, and had jostled his lordship's arm at the last moment, which was why Amanda Colby was alive with a hole in her hat instead of dead with a hole in her brain.

Bluebell blundered headlong through the woods. Trees rushed past and a small moon lurched and weaved about the stormy sky above.

Amanda all but ran into Richard, who had come riding back hell for leather, after he had heard the shot.

"I'm all right," shouted Amanda. "Home! Let's get home."

Bluebell did not slow until the tall chimneys of Fox End came in sight. Then he dug in all four hooves and began cropping some plants by the side of the road.

"Leave him!" hissed Richard.

"I can't," wailed Amanda. "There are a lot of donkeys around here, but one who has recently been ridden and standing at a place so near Fern Hill would bring suspicion down on our heads. Get some sugar."

"I have some in my pocket," said Richard. He held

it out and Bluebell immediately started trotting obedi-
ently after Richard's horse.

They did not speak until they had unsaddled the
animals, rubbed them down, and put them in their
respective stalls for the night.

Then they sat down in the harness room, and, by the
light of one candle, prised open the lid of the jewel
box. Diamonds, pearls, rubies, and emeralds sparkled
and blazed up into their wide, shocked eyes. Richard
silently drew out Lord Hawksborough's large ruby ring
and handed it to Amanda. It looked like a great drop of
glistening blood.

"I feel sick and dirty," said Richard, his voice seem-
ing to come from far away. "I meant to revenge you by
taking his ring."

White-faced, Amanda nodded and handed him back
the ring, which he dropped into the box with the other
jewels.

"We should never have done it," said Richard slowly.
"It was exciting at first, but frightening old men and
women is a terrible thing to do. Those servants were
too old to protect anybody. What was that shot?"

Amanda took off her tricorne and handed it to him.
There was a hole through the crown. "Lord Hawksborough," she said. "Bluebell would not move. He
climbed on the roof of the carriage. The coachman
jogged his arm or I should not be alive,"

"What will we do?" said Richard, his voice hoarse
with the effort of holding back tears. "I don't want the
jewels. I don't want any of it."

He looked very young and vulnerable. Amanda took
his hand in hers. "We'll bury them in the earth of the
stable floor," she said. "And if we ever get a chance to

go to London, we'll dig them up and leave them at Lord Hawksborough's house. Oh, I wish I were dead."

Richard shivered. "If you could have seen the look on his face, Amanda. He would have killed me with his bare hands if he had not been concerned over the welfare of his mother and sister. Vengeance, that's what he wants. And he won't rest till he gets it."

"Any minute now the search will be on," said Amanda urgently. "Fetch a pick and spade, Richard, and let us get finished with this terrible evening."

Richard worked like a man possessed, hacking and digging at the hard-packed earth of the stable floor until there was a sizable hole.

They wrapped the jewel box carefully in the sack, threw the tricornes, wigs, and masks on top of it, and piled the earth back in, stamped it down, and covered it with straw. Richard dusted his hands and gave a sigh of relief. "I feel a little better, but not much. Oh, Amanda, you and your crazy ideas."

"At least I have some ideas, crazy or not . . ." began Amanda hotly, and then she looked at her brother, her eyes glittering with unshed tears, and said, "Don't let's quarrel, Richard. We are *both* fools. I feel so terribly guilty."

"Aunt Matilda!" exclaimed Richard. "I think I hear her calling." He buttoned up his coat, saying urgently, "She must not find you in boy's clothes. I will go and talk to her while you go in by the kitchen door and change."

Amanda did as she was bid, tearing off the clothes in her bedroom and stuffing them into the back of a closet.

When she pushed open the door of the morning

room it was to find Richard waiting impatiently by the fire while Aunt Matilda sat in one of the wing chairs, very upright, very excited.

"Now you are here, Amanda," she cried. "I would not tell my news until we were all together. You will never guess where I have been today. I have been at Hember Cross for a meeting with my old school friend, Maria Pitts!"

"Well, that was very pleasant, I'm sure," said Amanda, wondering if she dared send Richard to fetch the rest of the brandy.

"But it is better than that!" cried Aunt Matilda. "You see, I heard she would be staying at the Feathers, although she did not attend the ball. I called on her and told her of our plight. I would not have found the courage to be so pushing for myself, but I consider you both my children, and you shall not starve as long as there is breath in this body," said Aunt Matilda, striking her scrawny bosom.

Richard and Amanda looked away with all the customary embarrassment the young feel when confronted by the old making a cake of themselves.

"Maria was vastly fond of me when we were at school and she immediately offered us *all* a home in London. She said Amanda would be a very good friend for her daughter, who is to make her come-out next Season, and she was sure something could be found for Richard.

"We are to advertise Fox End and let it to some suitable party, and then we are to go to London, and . . . Oh, it is the first and only really sensible thing I have done in my life."

Amanda and Richard forced themselves to congratulate their aunt and make a fuss over her, but each was thinking that this terrible evening need never have happened and Aunt Matilda's good news was only burying them under a greater weight of guilt.

"When are we to leave?" asked Amanda at last.

"As soon as someone can be found to take Fox End. I called at Mrs. Jolly's on the road home and she thinks it will do very well for her cousin, and she thinks he will be free to take it in a month or two."

"How did you get to Hember Cross?" asked Richard.

"I walked," said Aunt Matilda.

"You're a Trojan, Aunt," said Richard. Hember Cross was ten miles from Fox End.

Almost at the same time, Amanda and Richard began to feel more cheerful. The same thought had struck them. If they were to live in London, they could take the jewels with them and get the wretched stuff back to its rightful owner.

"But, Aunt," said Amanda slowly, "we have not the clothes for a London Season."

"That is to be arranged as well," cried Aunt Matilda. "Maria is amazingly generous."

"Mrs. Pitts must be very fond of you."

"Oh, she is. Nobody else liked her. The other girls found her too severe and moralising. But no one wanted to be my friend either, because I was quite poor and very timid, and so we found we had each other. She did say, as I recall, that she would never forget me and if I were in need of any help, she would always be there. We exchanged a few letters and then she ceased to write altogether. Someone at the ball who had known me slightly a long time ago told me that my friend Maria was to stay a night at the Feathers *en route* for London.

"But I forgot to tell you the other piece of excitement.

All the men in the neighbourhood have been rounded up to try to track down two monstrous highwaymen who robbed a coach on Fern Hill. It is amazing they did not come for you, Richard."

"Why should they come for me?" cried Richard, turning pale.

Aunt Matilda looked at him in amazement. "Because you are an able-bodied man, dear Richard. But possibly it is because Mr. Brotherington was called to help organise things, and, well . . . he does not approve of any of us."

"Did they call at the vicarage?" asked Amanda.

"Oh, yes, the squire did to see if the Jollys had seen or heard anything. Two highwaymen it was, one on a donkey and one on a horse, he said. One large and one small. 'Do you know,' I said, 'that sounds just like Richard and Amanda,' and how the squire did laugh!"

"I'll get the brandy," said Amanda abruptly.

Aunt Matilda watched her go, an anxious frown creasing her forehead. "I trust our dear Amanda is not taking to strong spirits, Richard?"

"No, she is excited about your good news," said Richard, who still looked very pale. "Have you thought, Aunt, that we cannot live on Mrs. Pitt's generosity forever?"

"Of course not. Just until the Season is over. Mrs. Pitts says she will find a husband for Amanda. She says if she can find a husband for her own daughter, then she can find a husband for *anyone*," added Aunt Matilda with a giggle.

What an unkind thing to say, thought Richard.

"And," Aunt Matilda was going on, "if our dear

Amanda does not *take,* we will still have Fox End and we will have the rent from Mrs. Jolly's cousin."

Richard brightened. A vision of his future raced through his head. Go to London . . . return the jewels . . . disguise himself and hand 'em to Lord Hawksborough's servant . . . Amanda would not have to worry about getting married . . . a good sort but not exactly a beauty to bring the suitors crowding around . . . back home to hunting and fishing and perhaps the arms of Miss Belinda Tring-Carter.

He thought briefly of the saucy girl he had kissed in the seminary garden. No, she had been too bold. He liked women to be gentle and meek and helpless.

Amanda returned with the brandy and three glasses.

She still looked tired and strained so Richard hurriedly pointed out that they could return to Fox End after the Season next July and find the rent from Mrs. Jolly's cousin waiting to carry them through a good few months until such time as he fashioned a career for himself.

Amanda gradually began to look less strained. Perhaps she would meet a pleasant young man during the Season who would want her as a bride. Someone who did not enrage her and leave her feeling strangely breathless as Lord Hawksborough had done. Someone with whom she could be comfortable.

Then she remembered the call from Mr. Brotherington's servant, and told Richard she was sure their persecution had only just begun.

"He can't persecute us when we ain't here." Richard grinned.

"And Mr. Jolly's cousin is a retired judge," said

Aunt Matilda. "He'll probably have him up at the next assizes."

Amanda looked wonderingly at her aunt. The change from the sad, drooping, depressed female of before the assembly was amazing. Aunt Matilda positively sparkled.

Then Amanda's thoughts went on to the mysterious Mrs. Pitts. She did not sound at all as if she would turn out to be a companionable woman. But perhaps her daughter was better. Amanda had never had a female friend. And then something Mrs. Jolly once said about Aunt Matilda came back to her. "Your aunt," Mrs. Jolly had said one day, "was not always so quiet and timid. She was companion to a horrible old lady at one time, a Mrs. Hersey, who bullied her unmercifully. But strange to say, your aunt seemed to blossom under the treatment. She really needs someone to tell her what to do every minute of the day."

Oh, dear, thought Amanda, does that mean Mrs. Pitts is a bully?

Then she found her eyes beginning to droop with the effects of the brandy and the emotional strain of the day.

When she finally lay down to sleep, she found herself dreaming of a secure and comfortable life, free from the threat of poverty, and free from the necessity of marrying the first man who asked her.

4

It was a bare month after the highway robbery that the Colbys and Aunt Matilda found themselves ready to leave for London. Mrs. Jolly's cousin, a Mr. Cartwright-Browne, had been told by his physician that he should spend some time in the country to ease the pressure of his blood. He was due to take up residence a week after the Colbys left.

Amanda and Richard had decided to unearth the box of jewels and burn the masks and hats and wigs on the bonfire an hour before they left. They could not risk doing it sooner in case they were surprised by Aunt Matilda, who had lost her need for long, escaping sleep and woke at the slightest sound.

Mrs. Pitts's generosity did not run to furnishing them with a carriage to take them to London and so they were taking the vicarage carriage into Hember Cross and from Hember Cross they were to catch the mail coach to London, an expensive mode of travel which would take almost the last of their money.

But this mode of travel had the advantage of speed. They could leave in the morning and arrive in London

in the afternoon, thereby saving the greater expense of a
night at a posting house.

The trunks were corded and ready, the furniture had
been swathed in holland covers to keep the dust from it
until Mr. Cartwright-Browne should arrive, and Aunt
Matilda was up in her room fussing over the packing of
toiletries into two handboxes when Amanda and Richard made their way silently to the stables.

"I'll feel a million times easier when we have the
jewels with us," said Richard. "I kept a small trunk
just for the purpose to slip in with the others in the
hall."

"Don't talk so loudly," whispered Amanda. "Oh,
what is that?"

There was a rumble of carriage wheels in the drive at
the front of the house.

"Let Aunt see to whoever it is," said Richard urgently.
"We must have the jewels."

But before they could reach the stables, the carriage,
instead of stopping at the front of the house, drove
right around the side and halted beside them. It was
the carriage from the vicarage. An elderly gentleman
opened the door and stiffly climbed down.

"You must be the Colby twins," he said. "Allow me
to introduce myself. I am Mr. Cartwright-Browne."

He was a very old gentleman, small and wizened, in
a pepper-and-salt frock coat and gaiters. He wore a
bagwig and carried a cane.

Richard signalled to Amanda with his eyes. "Please
step into the house, Mr. Cartwright-Browne," she said.
"I will find you some refreshment. You were not expected until next week."

"That I know, Miss Colby, but Mrs. Jolly—I arrived

there last night—told me you were leaving this morning. I decided to move in right away. I am very fond of my cousin but I have always lived alone and am set in my ways. I would like to see the stables first.

"I believe you are leaving a horse and a donkey in my charge? Good. They will be well looked after. I have sent for my servants and they will be arriving later today."

"But . . ." began Richard desperately, but Mr. Cartwright-Browne was already marching towards the stables with a quick, rather crablike gait.

Richard threw a wild look at Amanda, and both followed.

Mr. Cartwright-Browne examined the stables and the harness room, and then gave Bluebell a lump of sugar and stroked his nose. The minutes ticked by and still the old gentleman prodded this and that with his cane and asked innumerable questions.

"If we could finish this conversation in the house . . ." Amanda was beginning to say, when a shadow fell across them. The bulk of Mr. Brotherington looked in the doorway.

"Heard there was a new tenant," he said, striding forward. "I own all the land about here. I'll have you know I'll shoot that donkey if I find it on my pasture again, see."

"Who are you?" snapped Mr. Cartwright-Browne.

"Name of Brotherington."

"Well, Brotherington," said Mr. Cartwright-Browne, very stiffly on his stiffs. "I am the new tenant. My name is Mr. Cartwright-Browne. *You* are trespassing on *my* property and if you don't take yourself off, I shall have you taken to the nearest roundhouse and charged."

"Ho!" Mr. Brotherington tried to stare Mr. Cartwright-Browne down, but harder and wickeder men had tried when they had faced up to the elderly judge from the dock of the Old Bailey.

"Don't say I didn't warn you," snarled Mr. Brotherington, walking away stiff-legged like a surly bulldog being outfaced by a fox terrier.

"I shall see to that man before very long," said Mr. Cartwright-Browne meditatively, and if the twins had not been so worried about the jewels, they would have enjoyed the prospect of looking forward to hearing about how their tormentor was being tormented.

"Amanda! Richard!" called Aunt Matilda. "Oh, there you are!"

Introductions were made. "Jem coachman is anxious to be on his way," said Aunt Matilda, once the formalities were over. "He says the roads are treacherous and we should take advantage of the early start if we are to meet the mail. But I feel we should take Mr. Cartwright-Browne over Fox End before we leave."

"Indeed, yes," chorused Richard and Amanda.

"No need for that, ma'am," said the old gentleman. "Mrs. Jolly says she knows your house as well as she knows her own and she will be calling later to put me in the way of things."

In vain did Amanda and Richard protest. In vain did Amanda try to delay their departure by inventing missing fans and bonnets. Mr. Cartwright-Browne stood smiling outside the stables and it seemed as if he were set to stay there all day.

"I'll find some way of riding back from town and getting them," whispered Richard to Amanda at last. "We can't stay any longer."

And with that, Amanda had to be satisfied.

The vicarage coach rumbled forward. Amanda craned her neck until the tall chimneys of Fox End had vanished from sight. They were headed for London and the uncertain future, and the unknown Mrs. Pitts and her daughter.

They made a fairly silent journey of it. Aunt Matilda had suddenly lost all her vigour, and slept most of the way.

After the mail coach had deposited them in the City, Richard commandeered a hack. "Where to?" he asked Aunt Matilda.

She opened her reticule and fumbled around until she found a small pair of steel spectacles, which she balanced on the end of her long pink nose. Then she scrabbled and fumbled again, spilling out papier poudre, a vinaigrette, a lead pencil, a box of lucifers, a whole forest of bone pins, two combs, and a steel looking glass, before she found a slip of paper. "Oh, here it is," she sighed. "Berkeley Square. Number five."

"Are you sure?" asked Richard. "That is one of the most fashionable addresses in London."

"Quite sure," said Aunt Matilda. "Mrs. Pitts wrote it down for me herself."

Amanda climbed into the hack, wrapping her skirts around her ankles to keep them clear of the dirty straw on the floor. She felt no excitement at being in London. She felt deafened by the noise and bustle.

Postmen in scarlet coats with bells and bags were going from door to door; porterhouse boys were running with pewter mugs of beer for the evening's suppers; small chimney sweeps with gigantic brushes were wearily trudging home; bakers were calling "Hot loaves," their raucous voices competing with the bells of the dust carts and the horns of the news vendors. Apprentices were chattering and shouting to each other as they put up the heavy shutters on the bow-fronted, multi-paned windows of their masters' shops; ragged urchins were leapfrogging over posts; and hawkers with bandboxes on poles were threading their way through the jostling crowd.

There were vast hooded wagons with wheels like rollers, and brewers' drays drawn by Suffolk Punches, those huge and powerful draught-horses; bullocks on their way back from Smithfield wandering into yards, and rickety hackney coaches with their ancient jehus, like the one bearing Amanda out of the City and towards the West End of London.

Every house seemed to have the same unadorned face of freestone-bordered sash, the same neat pillars on either side of the pedimented door, the same stone steps over the area crowned by a lamppost.

They made their way along Cheapside to Newgate Street and then along Holborn, from Holborn to Oxford Street, and then from Oxford Street through Hanover Square. Now that they were in the West End, the London of fashion, bounded by Grosvenor Square and St. James's Square, Amanda could see signs of wealth all around in the carefully ordered streets and the huge town houses and in the very absence of bustle which had so marked the rest of the capital that she had driven through.

Berkeley Square was reached all too soon for Amanda, who had become increasingly nervous. Her plain muslin gown and nankeen pelisse and Pamela bonnet seemed increasingly countrified.

And why had she never noticed before how shiny with wear Richard's morning clothes had become.

Fortunately for Amanda, night had fallen, and her first sight of the town mansion which was to be her home in the succeeding months was no more than a vague impression of a vast, square bulk. And so she was able to convince herself that Mrs. Pitts surely rented a genteel flat among other genteel flats. No one could possibly live in the whole thing.

A footman in scarlet-and-silver livery with silver epaulettes opened the door, looking every bit as grand as a Hussar officer.

"Miss Pettifor and Mr. and Miss Colby, guests of Mrs. Pitts," said Aunt Matilda.

"There is no lady of that name resident here," said the footman, his quick eyes flicking up and down their countrified dress. He made a move to close the door.

"But you must be mistaken," said Aunt Matilda, beginning to cry noisily. "You *must*. We have come so far, and Maria wrote this address down for me herself."

"What is it, James?" demanded another voice. The footman stood aside, and an imposing butler surveyed the small party on the doorstep.

"My aunt wishes to see Mrs. Pitts," said Amanda, throwing an irritated look at the now crumpled and sobbing Aunt Matilda. "But it is quite clear she has been given the wrong address."

"You are Miss Pettifor and Master and Miss Colby?" asked the butler, his face clearing.

Aunt Matilda stopped crying immediately. "Yes, indeed," she said, peering at him over the edge of a damp handkerchief.

He stood aside. "Then you are expected. Come this way. Mrs. Fitzgerald's maiden name was *Miss* Pitts."

"Of *course!*" cried Aunt Matilda, failing to notice the look of alarm on the twins' faces. "How silly of me! I remember she married, but I could not remember the gentleman's name."

Amanda and Richard shuffled nervously in behind Aunt Matilda, trying not to gawk at the magnificence of the entrance hall with its black-and-white tiles below and its painted ceiling above, which simulated an open sky with flying birds.

"The family is in the Red Drawing Room," announced the butler, throwing open a handsome pair of double doors and announcing the visitors in a loud ringing voice.

Mrs. Fitzgerald arose and walked forward to meet them. Her eyes, so like her son's, were pale and expressionless. She had a heavy jaw and a rather dumpy figure. Her hair was hidden under an elaborate lace cap.

"My dear Matilda!" she said in the sort of resounding voice that is used to making its presence felt in marble halls. "Susan, come forward and make your curtsy."

A thin, tall, dark girl with a very hard face in one so young, and thick black hair which she tossed from side to side, made an awkward curtsy, gave them an unsmiling look, and promptly retreated back to a sofa in a corner of the room.

Amanda took a deep breath. At least the sinister Lord Hawksborough was not present. With any luck, he did not live with his mother.

Mrs. Fitzgerald drew Aunt Matilda down beside her on a sofa in front of the fire and proceeded to organise that lady's life.

"Now, Matilda," she said, "in a moment I will ring for our housekeeper, Mrs. Renfrew, who will show you to your rooms. Dinner is at seven. I hope you will not find our town hours too late. I will lend you a gown, since I am sure you have nothing suitable. We planned a quiet evening, as it is your first. After dinner, we will play cards. My daughter and Amanda will become better acquainted."

Amanda and Richard looked hopefully towards Susan, who stared insolently back and then pointedly looked away.

Mrs. Fitzgerald's incisive voice went on and on. Aunt Matilda murmured "yes" and "no" like an obedient child.

The Red Drawing Room was vast. A Murillo depicting a religious scene—looted by the French from a Spanish church and rescued by Lord Hawksborough, as Amanda was to learn later—hung over the fireplace.

The rosewood and satinwood furniture was carved with a peacock design. There were also walnut pier tables. Enormous pier glasses ornamented two of the walls, topped with gold heads of Bacchus. The carpets had been woven with a coat of arms.

On two gilt console tables stood pairs of bronze and ormolu candelabra, their tall wax candles throwing a clear light over the room.

A pair of armchairs with Egyptian heads supporting the armrests, possibly made by the Royal upholsterers, Morel and Seddon, flanked the fireplace, which was ornamented with an overmantel of Chinese Chippendale.

Amanda and Richard sat down gingerly on two satinwood chairs near the door.

"This is *awful*," whispered Amanda. "I think I am

going to be bullied to death. And what are we to do about the jewels?"

"Well, at least we know where to bring them," said Richard. "Let's hope Hawksborough lives somewhere else. He looked at me so long and hard that night, Amanda, I could swear he could see right through my disguise."

"Listen!" said Amanda. "Mrs. Fitzgerald is talking about the robbery."

"No!" Aunt Matilda was exclaiming. "To think you, dear Maria, were being robbed by these ruffians, only shortly after I left you. I did not think it could possibly be you because I saw you at Hember Cross such a little while before and you said you were going to Bellingham."

"My son was staying at the inn as well, and we both went directly to Bellingham after you left, and we only stopped for a few moments to pick up Susan."

"What a terrible ordeal," breathed Aunt Matilda. "You must have been monstrous frightened."

"I was so angry," said Maria Fitzgerald pugnaciously, "that I could not feel frightened. But Hawksborough will get those highwaymen, sooner or later."

"Hawksborough?" asked Aunt Matilda.

"My son," snapped Mrs. Fitzgerald. "You always had a brain like a peahen, Matilda."

"Of course," said Aunt Matilda, her face clearing. "Amanda told me that the excessively handsome man who took her in to supper was Lord Hawksborough. He was quite taken with her, you know. Then I thought . . . *Hawksborough,* where have I heard that name before? And then I remembered someone saying he was your son and just then I remembered a lady we used to know in the old days telling me she had heard you were recently widowed and resident at the inn, and so—"

"And so you arrive looking for Mrs. Pitts. Really, Matilda, what *have* you got in that feather head of yours? When the highway robbery occurred, did not the whole countryside tell you that we had been robbed and tell you our name?"

"There wasn't much time," pleaded Aunt Matilda, "and apart from Mrs. Jolly, who is really too worried about the health of her five children at the moment to think of much else, we didn't really *see* anyone else, except, of course, Mrs. Jolly's cousin, who has leased the house."

"And what is this, pray, about Hawksborough being 'taken' with Amanda?" demanded Mrs. Fitzgerald. "He told me he had a most boring time in the country, and I am sure I told him you and the Colbys were coming on a visit, and he did not mention he had met your daughter before. Furthermore, he has just become engaged to a most suitable female, Lady Mary Dane. He never ran after little girls as far as I can remember."

"So that puts *you* in your place, Amanda," announced Susan Fitzgerald with a surprisingly attractive ripple of laughter.

Mrs. Fitzgerald paid absolutely no heed to her daughter's interruption. "You will have the honour of meeting Lady Mary later. She is staying with us at present." The Colbys were to learn that Lady Mary stayed more at Berkeley Square than she did in her own home. "Mrs. Renfrew will now take you to your rooms. Susan, do you wish to go above with Amanda and become better acquainted?"

"No."

"Very well," said Mrs. Fitzgerald equably. She rang the bell and delivered them over to a stern matron in black bombazine.

Richard stumbled awkwardly against a chair in his rush to hold the doors open for his aunt and Amanda, and Susan laughed again.

They followed the housekeeper up the long curved staircase which led to the upper floors. On the second floor, the housekeeper ushered Aunt Matilda into one room, and then, walking a little farther along the corridor, pushed open another and indicated to Amanda that she had arrived at *her* room. Then with another little jerk of her head, the housekeeper signalled to Richard that he was to follow her.

Amanda went inside and shut the door and leaned against it. If only Fox End had not been let to Mr. Cartwright-Browne! Otherwise she would have run away that very evening.

She looked around the room with wide eyes.

It was dominated by a heavy four-poster of the Queen Anne period with a wrought-cloth canopy. The hangings were of heavy cloth in green and gold. The bed was so high, a short flight of steps led up to it. Beside the bed stood a night commode. There was a tallboy, a writing bureau, a small chest of drawers, a dressing table draped with chintz, and a swing looking glass. There were also three chairs and a small toilet stand.

Beside the bed was the inevitable tin rushlight canister pierced with holes.

She moved slowly forward. A small fire of sea coal crackled busily on the shining hearth. The toilet table boasted both Joppa and Windsor soap.

The dressing table was crowded with fascinating-looking bottles and tins. There was tooth powder, and face powder, and lip salves. A selection of choice perfumes had been neatly lined up as if for inspection—Spirit of Ambegris, Otto of Roses, Aqua Mellis, and Cordova Water. A set of tortoiseshell hairbrushes, obviously new, lay ready for use.

Mrs. Fitzgerald is very patronising and domineering, thought Amanda, but our hostess has certainly spent a deal of money to make us comfortable.

She sat down at the dressing table after removing her bonnet and pelisse.

So Lord Hawksborough was to be married. And she, Amanda Colby, had made so little impression on him that he had not even remembered her name.

I'm *glad* we took the jewels and I'm *glad* Richard took his wretched ring, Amanda thought fiercely. But all the old guilt for what they had done, memories of their terrible criminal deed, came back stronger than ever before, and all she wanted to do was to run as far away from London as possible.

The door swung open and Susan strode in and threw a pile of clothes on the bed. "Mathers will be along to fix you up," she said, and turned on her heel.

"Stay!" cried Amanda. "Who is Mathers?"

"My lady's maid, of course," snapped Susan. "Don't you know *anything*?" And with that, she stumped out.

What a horrible girl, thought Amanda. And I had so hoped for a friend.

The maid, Mathers, then arrived. Amanda felt extremely embarrassed and awkward at having to reveal herself to anyone in such shabby underwear, but the maid was too well-trained to make any comment. She was so placid and silent, in fact, that Amanda began to relax and to enjoy being pinned and dressed and groomed.

"There you are, Miss Colby," said the maid an hour later, speaking for the first time. "I'll send a footman to escort you downstairs. The family meets in the Green Drawing Room on the ground floor before dinner. They always use the state apartments whether they've got company or not."

She curtsied and left.

Amanda walked slowly to the looking glass, praying for a transformation, hoping to see she had miraculously become a plump, well-rounded debutante with rosy cheeks and shining eyes.

But her reflection told her that she still looked as if she did not belong in society.

Her gown was very plain, being of a peculiarly dull violet color. Her hair had been braided into a small crown and threaded with silk violets with green silk leaves. Amanda gathered that the gown had been one of Susan's and wondered at Mrs. Fitzgerald choosing such an *aging* color for her daughter.

Amanda decided to use a little of the scent and picked up the glass bottle of Otto of Roses. Just then, a footman scratched at the door and announced he had come to escort her downstairs. Amanda nervously spilled some of the scent over her arm, and, with an exclamation of dismay, hurriedly pulled on her old white gloves, seized the gold silk stole Aunt Matilda had made for her, and followed the footman down the stairs.

The Green Drawing Room was as vast as the Red. It was no longer green, having been redecorated in gold and red stripes. It was chilly, since the fire had only recently been lit. Amanda accepted a glass of wine from a footman and turned to look for Richard. He entered behind her, appearing much older and more assured then he had been earlier. He was wearing the suit of evening clothes he had worn to the ball, but his cravat was impeccably tied and his hair had been teased into artistic disorder.

"You look very fine," whispered Amanda.

"Got Hawksborough's valet sent to attend me. Oh, lor', Amanda, Hawksborough *lives* here!"

"Stop whispering!" shouted Susan Fitzgerald. "It's rude."

The now less intimidated Colbys, fortified with wine, looked at her with dislike.

Susan was wearing a white muslin gown, cut low enough to reveal more of her angular, bony body than Amanda felt was decent. Her black hair was dressed wih an elaborate confection of flowers and jewels.

Aunt Matilda was attired in scarlet merino with black stripes, making Amanda wonder if the Fitzgeralds were getting rid of all their unsuitable clothes by giving them to their guests.

The next arrival was an extremely handsome woman in her late twenties. She was wearing a white evening dress of leno, a thin linen fabric worked in the Etruscan pattern, cut low at the back and worn high in the front. The back was drawn and finished with a loose bow ornamented with footing lace. On her blonde hair she wore a headdress of white satin, ornamented with flowers.

She had very bright blue eyes and that breezy, unaffected manner which is often assumed by people who are in fact extremely affected.

"Lady Mary Dane," announced the butler as she swept into the room.

This, then, was Lord Hawksborough's fiancée.

Mrs. Fitzgerald performed the introductions. Susan, to Amanda's surprise, made an attempt at cordiality, even going so far as to compliment Lady Mary on her gown.

Lady Mary's bright blue gaze rested for a long moment on Richard, flicked over Amanda, and then settled on Aunt Matilda.

"You must be Mrs. Fitzgerald's old school friend," she cried, holding out both hands to Aunt Matilda. "Are you not fatigued after your journey?"

"I . . ." began Aunt Matilda, but Lady Mary had already swung around. "Charles!" she exclaimed.

Lord Hawksborough walked into the room. Amanda drew in her breath. Beside her, she could sense Richard's stillness.

Lord Hawksborough raised Lady Mary's hand to his lips. He was in full evening dress, looking much more magnificent than the last time Amanda had seen him. Even his eyes seemed different, she thought, seeing the amused warmth in them as he looked about the room.

Without the bad-tempered expression which had marred his features at the assembly, he appeared an extremely handsome, vital, and attractive man.

He was introduced to Aunt Matilda and then he turned to face the Colbys.

The silver eyes blinked a little as he looked at Amanda. Amanda felt very dowdy and insignificant beside the other ladies.

Lord Hawksborough was still looking at her and he

was beginning to frown. Amanda's heart missed a beat and she moved a little closer to her brother.

It's that girl from the assembly, Lord Hawksborough was thinking. Colby, of course. And this Richard is her brother!

He saw the familiar turn of her head and the way the elegance of her London hairstyle set off the proud shape of it. He saw the translucence of her skin, complimented by the dark stuff of her gown. He saw the strange gold-flecked eyes with their wary, watching look. He thought she looked enchanting.

Feeling increasingly plain and dowdy, Amanda dropped a curtsy.

"Miss Amanda," he said, smiling into her eyes. "We have met. How could I forget you? No one has noticed my leg since. And this is Richard, your brother? There I was at that wretched, boring assembly, pining away because I thought he was your country swain. You cannot conceive the agonies of jealousy that racked my poor frame."

Lady Mary took his arm in a possessive grip and smiled at Amanda in a kind of brittle way. "Pay no attention to Charles," she said. "He is always breaking the hearts of little girls with his empty compliments."

Lord Hawksborough glanced at his fiancée.

He was about to give her a set-down by saying he had meant every word of it. But he was about to be married, and his flirting with Miss Colby had been insulting to his future bride.

He gave Lady Mary's hand a warm squeeze. "You know me very well." He laughed, leading her towards the fire.

"As if you would look at *her* when you've got Lady

Mary," said Susan. Susan gave Lady Mary a fawning
look and Amanda thought with irritation: She has a
schoolgirl adoration of Lady Mary.

Lord Hawksborough turned around and glared at
Susan. "You were sent to that seminary against my
wishes. We could well have afforded a governess for
you, but Mother said the company of other girls would
humanize you. The experiment seems to have failed
miserably. Try for a little courtesy."

Susan flushed to the roots of her hair, and Amanda
found herself almost sorry for the girl.

Dinner was announced.

Amanda was by now not surprised to find that Mrs.
Fitzgerald had chosen the state dining room for dinner,
rather than settling for one of the smaller family dining
rooms.

Dinner was a long and awkward meal. They were all
seated so far away from each other that conversation had
to be carried on at the pitch of the voice.

The only ones this seemed to trouble were Amanda,
Richard, and Aunt Matilda. Lord Hawksborough and
Lady Mary seemed to be able to make their voices carry
without bothering to shout, and mother and sister
talked in very loud voices even when they didn't have
to.

At last the ladies arose to leave the gentlemen to
their wine, the only gentlemen being Richard and Lord
Hawksborough. The viscount noticed the nervous, almost warning look Amanda threw her brother before
she left the room. He assumed Richard might not be
able to carry his wine.

Amanda suffered the tortures of the damned waiting
for the gentlemen to join the ladies. What if Richard's

conscience got the better of him and he blurted out the whole story?

But when they returned, after what seemed like a terribly long time to Amanda, Richard looked happy and excited and Lord Hawksborough urbane and amused.

Susan was pressed by Mrs. Fitzgerald to entertain the company, which she finally did with bad grace. She plumped herself down at the flat harpsichord-pianoforte and started to play "The Woodpecker" with amazing verve and quite terrible inaccuracy.

The muslin of her gown and petticoat had become caught on the edge of the piano stool so that Susan was exposing an unmaidenly length of hairy, muscular leg encased in a flesh-colored stocking. "I must tell her to pull her gown down," whispered Amanda to Richard. "No one else is going to trouble."

"Never mind her wretched legs. I say, she is a hairy 'un, ain't she?" said Richard, his voice tinged with awe. "You'll never guess what Hawksborough said to me!"

"What?" Amanda's attention was successfully diverted from Susan.

"He is sending me off to Oxford! Imagine! I am to live with his old tutor until I am ready to start the new term."

"Richard!" gasped Amanda, clinging to his arm and turning quite pale. "You cannot leave me. Take me with you."

"Don't *clutch*," said Richard crossly, shaking his arm free. "What's come over you, Amanda? You've got everything here a girl could possibly desire."

"How *can* you? How can you *say* such a thing? I am

to be left with that dreadful Susan and that awful Mrs. Fitzgerald. And what about the jewels?"

"Shhhh! Not so loud. Forget about the jewels. Don't you see? It will be easy for me to skip down from Oxford and pick them up and return them quietly. Hawksborough's a great gun, Amanda. I wish to goodness we had never done such a thing. And to think I took his ring! I only did it because you said he had been horrible to you. You're an awful liar, Amanda. He couldn't be awful to anyone."

"Richard!" gasped Amanda, white to the lips. "I don't *know* you. I don't know you *at all*."

"Stop talking fustian. Look, I'll write."

"When do you leave?"

"Tomorrow."

"You can't leave tomorrow. We've only just got here!"

"Stop saying *can't, can't, can't* in that maddening way. This old tutor of Hawksborough's happens to be leaving London tomorrow. I'm only going to Oxford."

Amanda shook her head in a dazed way. Never in her wildest dreams had she ever thought of Richard so selfishly abandoning her.

Mrs. Fitzgerald chose that moment to call for a game of whist, and Richard, anxious to ingratiate himself with his hosts and to get away from his demanding sister, eagerly offered to make up a four. Susan slammed the keys of the pianoforte in an angry way and then strode from the room.

Mrs. Fitzgerald was partnered by Aunt Matilda, and Richard was partnered by Lady Mary.

Lord Hawksborough strolled over to where Amanda

was sitting in the corner, his quick eyes taking in the pallor of her face and the slight trembling of her hands.

"Has young Colby told you his news?" he asked.

Amanda nodded. "It is all very sudden," she said in a low voice.

"It is a good opportunity. Are you frightened at being left alone in a strange house with . . . er . . . strange people?"

Amanda nodded again, and then shivered, for the room was cold.

"Come with me," he said. "We can talk more easily in the library. It is much warmer there."

"Won't Lady . . . won't anyone mind?" asked Amanda, looking over at the card players.

"No, why should they?" He offered her his arm as he had done at the assembly.

He led the way through the vast expanse of the cold hall and up the stairs to the first floor and into a large and pleasant library.

A cheerful fire blazed on the hearth and firelight flickered over the rows and rows of calf-bound volumes along the walls. He rang the bell and ordered wine and biscuits, and then settled Amanda in a chair by the fire and took the chair opposite.

"Now, Miss Amanda," he said, pouring her a glass of wine after the servant had left, "tell me your troubles. My mother is not so frightening as she appears. She *will* bully people if they let her. Susan is a great problem. I really don't know what is wrong with her. If Mother hopes to marry her this Season, then she has much more confidence in the attractions of a large dowry than I. Susan is rude and loud, but not malicious. So what made you so pale this evening?"

"It was when Richard told me he was leaving."

"You love your brother very much?"

"Yes. I don't know. I don't know anyone else, you see."

"Ah, now I remember. I gather that you have practically no money and that, if I recall what you said correctly, you had no social life."

"That is correct," said Amanda, looking away from him, because the interest and concern in his strange eyes were doing things to her breathing. She took a great gulp of wine and went on, "Richard and I did everything together. We went hunting and fishing and shooting. I did not go to school, but Richard did, and he taught me to read and write."

"You had better begin at the beginning," he said gently. "When did your parents die?"

And so Amanda did as she was bid, beginning to lean back in her chair and relax under the soothing effect of the wine, the heat from the fire, and his interest in her life.

It was a dreary little story, reflected the viscount with a stab of compassion: weeks and months and years of scrimping and saving with no friends or family other than a faded spinster aunt and a twin brother.

The firelight brought out the red and gold lights like little sparks in her hair and her eyes grew wider and darker as she became absorbed in her story.

When she had finished, he said quietly, "I think you would feel better about your situation here if you were to know that you had a certain measure of independence. My mother is inclined to be thoughtless, and would have you begging for every penny. She likes to be generous. She *is* generous. But she likes to exact friendship and affection in return. It is the only way she knows of getting it."

Amanda arched her brows in amazement at his candour. Did all people see their parents in such a detached way? Amanda could not remember her own.

"And so," he went on, "I shall see that an allowance is paid to you and we will furnish you with a dowry."

Amanda's eyes filled with tears. She remembered the jewels. She remembered his ruby ring and how it had blazed on his finger and how it was now under the stable floor.

She felt so miserable and guilt-ridden that she said, "You were not thus at the assembly! You seemed so hard . . . and . . . and I heard you tell the earl that you had never spent a more boring evening, and I heard you, and I wanted to sink through the floor with humiliation!"

"Oh, my wretched tongue," he said. "I am as bad as Susan. I did not mean you, my fairy. I meant the earl and his terrible food and his dreadful guests."

"But you looked so grim!"

He smiled at her anguished expression. "Indigestion, Miss Amanda. It was the first time I had ever suffered from it and I hope it may be the last. I had never had such filthy food as I was forced to eat at Hardforshire's."

"I cannot accept your generosity," wailed Amanda. "I will not *take*, you know."

"During the Season? Why on earth not?"

"Well, I am not exactly . . . well, Richard and Aunt Matilda are very kind about it but they do know that I am very plain. . . ."

"My dear child, you are the most enchanting creature I have seen in a long while. You have a very rare, elfin sort of beauty which is very captivating. I shall be beating your suitors from the door by the beginning of May."

"You are too kind," said Amanda in a stifled voice.

"I mean it. Did no one tell you you were beautiful before?"

Amanda dumbly shook her head.

"Then you are. I can see you do not believe me, but there will soon be plenty of other men to tell you so."

She looked at him, her whole face illuminated with happiness. He felt a strange pain in his chest and wondered if he was about to be cursed with a recurrence of indigestion.

"Thank you," breathed Amanda. "You have just given me a wonderful present." She darted from her chair and kissed him impulsively on the cheek.

"Oh," she said, blushing with confusion and subsiding back in her own chair again. "How very forward of me."

"Not at all," he said, his eyes enigmatic. "I am not averse to being kissed by pretty girls." His silver eyes lit up with a wicked glint. "Like to try again?"

"Oh, my lord, I really do not think Lady Mary—"

"No, of course not," he said quickly, wondering what there was about Miss Colby that gave him this overwhelming desire to flirt.

"Talking about Lady Mary," he went on, "she is to go into the country tomorrow and this is the last time I shall see her for a few weeks. I must make my way back and enjoy as much of her company as I can."

He rose to his feet.

"Could . . . do I have to go back?" asked Amanda.

"No, I will make your excuses for you." He walked

to the doorway and then hesitated. "I do not have any commitments tomorrow. After you say good-bye to your brother, I will show you a little of London if you would like."

With all my heart and soul, Amanda was about to say, but she managed to bite it back and say demurely, "I should like that above all things."

"Very well," he said. "Good night, Miss Colby."

After he had gone, Amanda pirouetted around the room, overwhelmed with joy about having a protector against the stern Mrs. Fitzgerald and the awkward Susan. But then she remembered those wretched jewels and wished it had all never happened. If only she could move the clock back to the night of the assembly.

She walked from the library and up to the second floor, trying to remember where her bedroom was.

As she passed a door, she heard noisy sounds of crying.

Susan!

Her hand went to the knob and then dropped. Whatever ailed Susan, Amanda was sure she would not tell a stranger like herself. She wandered along one corridor and then another until she found a servant trimming the lamps and asked him to show her the way.

With the optimism of youth, Amanda decided to forget about the jewels for the moment and simply enjoy the fact that although Richard was going away, she had already found another brother to replace him.

The brother being Lord Hawksborough.

5

Amanda was still hurt by Richard's callous unconcern and made a very formal good-bye to him the next morning. To her irritation, Richard was so excited, he did not even seem to notice.

Lord Hawksborough told Amanda to put on her warmest clothes because they would be riding in an open carriage. Mathers, the maid, was miraculously on hand to help her into a blue velvet carriage costume and a Cardinal mantle of black cloth lined and trimmed with white fur. A capote was placed on her head, that bonnet with the soft crown and a stiff brim framing the face. And wonder of wonders, she found herself the proud possessor of a new pair of York tan gloves, those buff-colored suede gloves which were fashionable wear for men and women alike.

Lord Hawksborough was waiting for her in the hall in a many-caped driving coat and with a curly-brimmed beaver set to a nicety on his black curls.

"Where are you going?" demanded Susan's voice from the first landing.

"I am taking Miss Colby for a drive," answered Lord Hawksborough.

"Then I am coming too. Wait for me!" shouted Susan.

Amanda looked like a child who has found its birthday has been forgotten.

"Would you rather she did not come?" asked Lord Hawksborough.

"No," lied Amanda. "I should like it above all things."

Susan was soon back wearing a lumpy pelisse over a high-ruffed morning gown. Her bonnet had such a huge poke that her face was invisible.

Amanda felt piqued and cross. She had imagined herself cutting a bit of a dash being escorted by the handsome viscount. Now the company of sulky Susan reduced the whole glory of the outing to a schoolgirl expedition.

Amanda had not slept well, which had soured her temper. Used to the quiet of the countryside, she found herself tossing and turning during the night as her ears were assaulted with the sounds of sleepless London.

The watchman, whose business was not merely to guard the streets and take charge of the public security, informed Berkeley Square every half-hour of the weather and the time. For the first three hours, Amanda was informed it was a moonlight night and all was well, at half-past three that it was a cloudy morning, and so on until six, when the stentorian voice of the watchman informed her that the sun was up. The rumble of the night coaches had scarcely ceased before the rattle of the morning carts began. Then came the dustman with his bell and his chant of "Dust-ho!"; then came the watchman again; then the porterhouse boy clattering pewter pots; then the milkman, and, among other cries, a shrill piercing voice selling fresh green peas.

Amanda was further annoyed to find that Susan had every intention of sitting bodkin between herself and Lord Hawksborough.

"Where are we going?" demanded Susan.

"All around the town," replied his lordship cheerfully with a flourish of his whip.

The light curricle moved off. Amanda tried to steal a look at Lord Hawksborough but found her view obstructed by Susan's enormous poke bonnet, which hung like a penthouse over her sulky face.

She decided to enjoy the view and pretend that Susan did not exist.

The morning's brief sun had disappeared and the winter's day was dark.

Amanda was bewildered by the amount of goods displayed in the shops and by the roar of the town.

The lower floors of the shops seemed to be made entirely of glass, with many thousands of candles lighting up silverware, engravings, books, clocks, glass, pewter, paintings, gold, precious stones, steelwork, and women's finery. There were endless coffee rooms and lottery shops. The apothecaries' windows glowed with giant bottles shining with purple, yellow, verdigris-green, or amber light. The confectioners' dazzled the eye with their candelabra shining over hanging festoons of Spanish grapes. Pretty shop girls in silk caps and little silk trains moved about among pyramids of cakes and oranges, tarts and pineapples.

The traffic was immense, the streets crowded with chaises, carriages, and drays. Above the hubbub of thousands of voices sounded chimes from the church towers, postmen's bells, organs, fiddles, hurdy-gurdies, tambourines, and the cries of the vendors selling hot and cold food at the street corners.

The very noise made conversation impossible, a fact Amanda would have regretted had not the taciturn Susan been present.

The viscount then threaded his way around and down to the shabby little ancient streets of Westminster, where they alighted and walked around the Abbey, looking at the sooty walls and crumbling monuments. From there they went to the Tower to see the King's jewels and the menagerie of wild animals; then to the British Museum beside Bloomsbury Fields to view the Parthenon marbles, recently brought from Athens. Back to the City, and the Royal Exchange with its piazza where foreigners in strange and wonderful costumes haggled with top-hatted Englishmen; and so to the Bank of England, where a private company of financiers was raising a handsome building behind high walls.

Lord Hawksborough seemed to know everyone everywhere he went. Amanda felt her head would burst trying to retain all the information she heard.

The only thing to mar the outing was the fact that everyone seemed to treat herself and Susan as schoolgirls his lordship was being gracious enough to entertain.

Lord Hawksborough treated them both to ices at Gunter's and then drove them back to Berkeley Square. Susan had hardly said a word during the whole tour.

When his lordship left the girls in the hall, Amanda followed Susan upstairs.

"Well, thank goodness that's over," said Susan, untying the strings of her poke bonnet.

"I wonder you bothered to come," remarked Amanda crossly.

Susan turned on the half-landing and gave Amanda a bright stare out of her black eyes. "I wanted to make sure Lady Mary's property was being guarded," she said with that quick toss of her black hair.

Amanda went scarlet, thinking of the jewels, thinking that Susan was calling her a thief.

"I am not in the habit of stealing!" said Amanda hotly.

"Then make sure you do not steal another woman's fiancé," retorted Susan, and stumped off down the corridor before Amanda had time to reply.

Amanda was furious, and then, as she went into her bedroom, her fury was replaced with a sort of comfortable glow. It was pleasant in a way to be regarded as dangerous where Lord Hawksborough was concerned, if only by his eccentric sister.

Amanda spent the next few minutes exploring the contents of her room more fully. She found a pristine diary in a drawer in the writing table, and after a moment's hesitation, sat down, and taking up a brass-nibbed pen, began to write about her tour around the sights of London, and then of all her worries about the robbery, and her hopes that Richard would find a way to restore the jewels.

When she had finished, she looked about for some place to hide the diary where it would not be found by the servants.

Finally she stood on a chair and put it on the top of the tallboy at the back where it could not be seen by anyone standing at floor level.

She dusted her hands and climbed down. The house

was very silent—silent now that her ears had become accustomed to the noises of the town outside.

Amanda decided to make her way to the library to see if she could find something to read.

She had a faint hope she might find Lord Hawksborough there so that perhaps they might talk without the company of angry Susan.

She was disappointed to find that although Lord Hawksborough was in the library, he was not alone.

"Come in, Miss Amanda," called the viscount as she hesitated in the doorway. "I would like you to meet the famous Bow Street Runner, Mr. Townsend. I feel sure he will catch those highwaymen for me."

Was it a trick of the light or had Miss Colby gone extremely pale? wondered Lord Hawksborough. But she came forward and dropped a curtsy, sending the Bow Street Runner a green sidelong look from under her lashes.

Mr. Townsend was a very smart, portly man, "clean as paint," to use his own expression. He wore a most peculiar costume. He was encased in a light and loud suit, knee breeches and short gaiters, and a white hat of great breadth of brim. In his hand he carried a tiny baton with a gilt crown on the top.

He acknowledged Amanda's curtsy with a clumsy bow and then turned to Lord Hawksborough to continue his conversation.

"So, as I was saying, my lord, I'll snaffle 'em for you. Wearing wigs, you think? And masks? I'll snaffle them coves and then get 'em to doff their sham phizzes, and we'll see who we've got for Jack Ketch. Drawing and quartering's too good for the likes o' them."

"Have . . . have you any idea who these villains might be?" asked Amanda in a sort of dry whisper.

"Not yet, my pretty," said the Runner, taking a sip from the glass of wine that Lord Hawksborough had handed him. "And that's odd," he went on, "for I thought I knew every kiddy on the High Toby lay. I thinks this is the work o' some lucky amateurs.

"Think, begging your lordship's permission, I'll take a journey down to that Hember Cross and sniff around."

Amanda sat down suddenly.

"Yes, Miss Colby," said Mr. Townsend, staring at her from under the sort of combined eaves of his flaxen wig and his large hat, "everyone who's anyone will tell you Townsend of Bow Street is the best. Two young noblemen came up to me one day near the palace, and one of these here sprigs says to the other, 'I will introduce you to old Townsend, I know him well. Come here, Townsend!' says he, with great hauteur, at the same time taking a pinch of snuff. 'I wish to ascertain a fact; but 'pon my honour, I do not intend to distress your feelings. In the early part of your life were you not a coal heaver?' 'Yes, my lord,' I answers, 'it is very true,' says I. 'But let me tell your lordship, if *you* had been reared up as a coal heaver, you would have remained a coal heaver up to the present hour.' "

"Very well, Townsend," said Lord Hawksborough, ignoring this tale, "you may go to Hember Cross with my blessing."

The Runner tossed off the rest of his wine and cast the viscount a sly look. "Very good wine, thank 'ee, my lord. Minds me of when I met the Duke of Clarence in St. James's Park. I told him, 'I am just come from your royal brother, who gave me two bottles of the best

wine.' 'Well,' says the duke, 'come and see me,
Townsend, and I promise to give you as good a bottle
as my brother York.' "

The Runner looked hopefully at Lord Hawksborough,
who rang the bell. "Hughes," he said to the butler.
"Please see that Mr. Townsend is given a few bottles of
burgundy."

Much gratified and with many promises to "get the
villains," the Runner took his leave.

"Come near the fire," said Lord Hawksborough, looking anxiously at Amanda. "You look cold and frightened.
You must not let old Townsend frighten you. He is a
great bag of wind. He has a reputation of being successful as a thief-taker, but I sometimes fear he is a bit of
an imposter."

"Do you hate those highwaymen so very much?"
asked Amanda in a low voice.

"My dear Miss Colby, I simply want legal vengeance.
I do not wish to strangle them with my bare hands
myself. I want them sentenced at the Old Bailey and
then dancing on the end of a rope."

Amanda's hand flew to her throat. "Perhaps they
were very hungry and had no money."

"Robbing honest citizens is a crime, Miss Amanda.
Let us talk of more pleasant things. Did you enjoy your
journey around the sights of London?"

"Oh, yes. Thank you," said Amanda, determined to
banish her fears for the moment.

"I hope to be able to entertain you a little this week,
Mis Amanda, before I take my leave. Do sit down."

"Take your leave?" echoed Amanda faintly. "Where?
Why?"

"I have certain business to conduct for the government of a delicate nature which involves travelling abroad."

"How long will you be gone?"

"A month or two. Do not look so stricken. You feel abandoned by your brother and now by me. But you will find my mother's bark is worse than her bite and she will set herself to entertain you royally. She has agreed to your allowance. As for Susan . . ." He frowned for a moment, turning his wineglass in his long fingers. "I am worried about Susan. She is a difficult child. She misses our father very much. He died when she was ten years old. Perhaps you might make an effort, Miss Colby, to find why she is so . . . er . . . prickly. You will do that for me?"

He smiled at her, a blinding smile, and Amanda felt she would do anything for him.

"I shall miss you," she said, her gold-tipped lashes veiling her eyes.

"Will you?" he teased. "How much, I wonder. Desperately? Passionately?"

"My lord—"

"I know, I should not speak so. I am an old bachelor and about to be an old married man."

"When? When will you be married?"

"I do not know, my elf. This year."

"You must be very much in love," said Amanda shyly.

There was a silence and she looked up at him quickly. His eyes were hooded. He sat very still, looking at the dregs of his wine.

"I admire and respect Lady Mary," he said at last.

"Is that enough?"

"You are impertinent, Miss Colby."

"I am sorry, my lord. I do not know much of the world. Perhaps I read too many romances. I had always hoped to marry for love."

"Then you may be one of the lucky ones." He sighed. "I had dinner with Lord Byron at Kinnaird's. He is to marry Miss Millbanke next month, you know, but I do not think the attachment is very romantic. Not what one would expect of a poet anyway. Kean was there—the famous actor. He is a marvellous raconteur.

"He told us that at Stroud in Gloucestershire, in *one* single night's performance, he acted Shylock, danced on the tightrope, sang a song called 'The Storm,' sparred with Mendoza, and acted Three-Fingered Jack. He said that one other night he forgot his part, and recited Milton's *Allegro* instead, without the audience appearing to notice the difference. Then he gave us imitations of Incledon, Kemble, Sinclair, and Master Betty, which were very fine. He said he could only act his part properly when acting with a pretty woman. I thought Byron would be encouraged to betray some warmth of feeling and talk about his love, but he never mentioned Miss Millbanke's name to us once."

"Is there such a thing as love?" asked Amanda boldly. "Or is it only in poems and books?"

"I think I am just becoming aware that such a thing might exist," he said with a wicked glint in his eye.

"Of course," said Amanda nervously. "Lady Mary is a very beautiful woman."

"And she is not here. But you are."

"My lord, you are flirting again. And let me tell you that your sister accompanied us today in order, as she put it, 'to protect Lady Mary's property.' "

"The devil she did!"

"I was very flattered," said Amanda primly. "I am not in the way of being considered a *femme fatale*."

"You will be," he said dryly. "I do not often behave so badly. If you set up in my respectable bosom this compulsion to flirt, I shudder to think of the effect you will have on less staid men."

"You do not look staid. You look . . . devilish."

"I preferred your earlier compliments, Miss Colby. I study my legs in the looking glass every day now and am become as vain of them as Mr. Romeo Coates is of his."

Amanda suddenly felt painfully shy. "Where is your mother, Mrs. Fitzgerald?" she asked.

"About the town with your aunt, making calls."

"And what do you do this evening, my lord?"

"I shall go to Watier's and gamble with the Pinks of the Ton. Why did you turn so pale when you saw Mr. Townsend?" he asked abruptly.

Oh, the jewels, thought Amanda wretchedly. Always the jewels! Oh, that she and Richard had never done such a thing. She hesitated, deciding at last to tell him the truth and throw herself on his mercy, deciding that she could not bear this great burden of guilt any longer.

"I think it was because he smells of the gallows," said the viscount, answering for her. "You must not be so softhearted, Miss Amanda. Such low villains are not worth your pity."

"What if . . . if they came to you and confessed?"

"They would need to be tried by court of law."

"Even if they were truly repentant?"

"This is hypothetical. Any men who will rob

defenceless women and old servants do not know the words remorse or pity."

"Oh," said Amanda dismally, her courage failing her.

"Do not look so sad. You think these low creatures are like yourself, with human feelings of compassion and conscience.

"Let me assure you, they are lower than animals! Now, to more pleasant things. I shall have a chance to dance with you once more. We have been invited to a ball at the Bartons' on Friday. Lord and Lady Barton are young and amusing. We have told them of your presence and you are now included in the invitation. Susan will no doubt find you something to wear. Most of society has gone to the country, but it will be a good opportunity for you and Susan to become accustomed to the ways of the world. And I have further intelligence to make your green eyes shine."

"Which is . . . ?"

"Richard Colby will be at the ball and will stay with you for the weekend before he returns again to Oxford."

"How wonderful!" said Amanda, although somehow the prospect of seeing Richard again did not fill her with any of the joy she felt it should.

"And now, if you will excuse me, Miss Amanda . . ."

He rose to his feet and Amanda rose hurriedly as well. He came to stand over her, so near her that she could feel the heat of his body.

He bent and raised her hand to his lips, turning it over at the last moment and pressing his lips to her wrist. Amanda felt a tingling sensation rushing up her arm and an aching sensation in the pit of her stomach.

He raised his eyes suddenly and looked down at her, wary and slightly surprised.

"Until later," he said softly. And then he was gone.

Amanda raised the wrist he had kissed and held it against her cheek. Then she became aware of what she was doing and abruptly dropped her arm, and, hearing the sound of her aunt's voice in the hall below, ran lightly down the stairs to meet her.

It transpired that both Susan and Amanda were to wear white for their first London ball, a white ball gown of Susan's being tucked and altered and shortened to fit Amanda.

Amanda was immensely pleased with her appearance for the first time in her life. If a man of the world like Lord Hawksborough found her attractive, then surely she must have a certain charm of which her aunt and her brother were completely unaware.

She had only had time to exchange a few words with Richard, who arrived from Oxford just in time to change into his evening dress.

Amanda nervously entered the Red Drawing Room wearing a ball gown of the thinnest white sarenet and white crêpe. White silk roses had been threaded into her carefully arranged hair, and she wore a new pair of white kid gloves.

Susan was in white silk, her dress being in the same fashionable high-waisted style as Amanda's. She wore red silk roses in her black hair, which had been dressed in an elaborate Grecian coiffure which added to her height and gave her tall figure a certain distinction.

"By George!" muttered Richard. "The prickly Miss Fitzgerald is in looks. I like a girl with character."

"I thought you liked them soft and feminine," teased Amanda.

"I think Miss Fitzgerald could be very feminine, given a chance," said Richard, looking at Susan with a speculative gleam in his eye.

Amanda followed his gaze and had to admit that at least Susan Fitzgerald for once looked relaxed and happy.

Mrs. Fitzgerald was soon to put an end to that.

Amanda, Richard, and Aunt Matilda were waiting for Lord Hawksborough to join them.

Aunt Matilda was nervous, her nose very pink and her hands constantly plucking at the folds of a new velvet gown. Amanda found her heart beating quickly, and her eyes kept sliding to the doors, waiting for the viscount to arrive. She had not seen him at all since that day in the library. She had told Richard about Townsend, the thief-taker, but Richard had adopted a man-about-town wordly air and had drawled that he had heard of the fellow, and it was said that Townsend was only capable of catching a thief who picked a pocket under his nose.

His manner irritated Amanda no end. Furthermore, Richard had not commented on her appearance and she still craved the admiration and approval of her twin.

"I met Liza Barrington this afternoon," said Mrs. Fitzgerald in her loud voice. "You know her daughter, Betty, Susan. She was at the seminary with you. Such a pretty little minx of a thing, and Liza has high hopes of marrying her off to a title. It is a pity you do not have the same roguish charm as Betty Barrington, Susan. 'Tis monstrous unfair that I should have such a plain daughter to puff off to the world."

Susan glared at the floor and hunched her shoulders.

"I think Susan looks very fine," said Amanda furiously. "Your own daughter, ma'am—!"

"Amanda. Respect your betters!" cried Aunt Matilda, her nose even pinker with distress.

Amanda bit her lip. Richard walked forward and took Susan's hand in his. She tried to snatch it away but he held it in a firm grip.

"You cannot speak for the gentlemen, Mrs. Fitzgerald," he said with a welcome return to his customary frank and open manner, "but *I* speak for the gentlemen, and I assure you Miss Susan has a certain air of character and distinction which is more attractive than the vapid simperings of many empty-headed debutantes."

Mrs. Fitzgerald looked furious, and then she shrugged and surveyed Richard as he stood holding Susan's hand with a certain glint of admiration in his eyes. "You knowing so many debutantes, of course," she said at last.

"Of course," said Richard mildly. Susan snatched her hand away and looked at him, a puzzled hurt look, a searching look at the same time, trying to find out if he were making a game of her.

Lord Hawksborough entered and Amanda's heart gave a lurch. He looked so handsome. I am as bad as Susan, Amanda immediately chided herself. I have a schoolgirl adoration of Lord Hawksborough just as Susan has one for Lady Mary.

Wraps and cloaks were collected and the party went out to the carriages which were to take them to the ball.

Aunt Matilda and the Colbys were to travel in one and the viscount and his mother and sister in the other.

"Well done," said Amanda, giving Richard's hand a squeeze.

"Susan?" He grinned. "Well, I meant it. No wonder she's so rough and sulky when her mother keeps telling her she's plain. I'll swear that was not the first time, you know."

"I do not see how my lord can have such a cruel mother," said Amanda, lowering her voice so that Aunt Matilda would not hear.

"As to that," said Richard thoughtfully, "you can't call her clutch-fisted or cruel so far as we are concerned. Susan doesn't stand up to her, that's the problem."

"You will dance with her," pleaded Amanda.

"I mean to," said Richard, and Amanda threw him a startled look in the darkness of the carriage.

Richard could surely not be forming a *tendre* for such a prickly nettle as Susan!

"Remember, Amanda," came Aunt Matilda's voice, "that you are to do *nothing* to embarass Mrs. Fitzgerald. Do *not* cross your legs, and do not speak unless you are spoken to. You must not refuse to stand up with *any* gentleman or that will mean you cannot dance with anyone else.

"And do not hold your fan by the handle. The fan should always be held at the *top* when you are not using it."

"Yes, Aunt," said Amanda meekly.

"It is a pity Lady Mary is not with us." Aunt Matilda sighed. "She and Lord Hawksborough would be a pleasure to watch. She is such a beautiful woman and with such free and easy manners. And so kind! He is a lucky man."

A good deal of Amanda's anticipation was dimmed. There was always something to mar the moment, she

thought crossly. If it was not those wretched jewels and
fear of arrest, it was listening to praise of Lady Mary.

They had only a short distance to travel to Lord and
Lady Barton's mansion, and Amanda wondered why
people insisted on travelling a few streets by carriage.
They had an hour to wait in the crush before they were
finally deposited at the door. Flambeaux in iron brack-
ets on the walls flared and spurted in the chilly air.

Sweet strains of music and the sound of dancing feet
brought a flush of anticipation to Amanda's pale face.
She was at her first London ball. Lord Hawksborough
was with her. And Lady Mary was not.

Amanda had dreamed of floating in Lord Hawksborough's arms to the strains of the waltz while envious
debutantes looked on. Sometimes Miss Devine would
be there, and in her dreams Amanda would throw her a
pitying look.

At first the evening promised to be something out of
a fairy tale. Thousands of scented candles blazed on
jewels and orders. The whole ballroom seemed a kaleido-
scope of color and movement. The thin stuff of the
ladies' gowns fluttered to the movement of the dance.
Diamonds caught fire under the glittering chandeliers.
Names that were previously known to Amanda only
through the social columns were murmured in her ear by
Aunt Matilda, who had picked up a remarkable fund of
gossip from the surrounding chaperones in the short
time since she had entered the ballroom.

"There's Mr. Brummell," whispered Aunt Matilda,
"and over there is Lady Jersey. The half-naked woman
is Lady Sefton. The Prince said she had a fine bust and
'tis said she has barely covered herself since, even in the

daytime. And there is Lord Byron with Lady Caroline Lamb, and beside him is his friend John Cam Hobhouse."

Amanda sat out only one dance. But Lord Hawksborough did not come near her. He seemed in high spirits and danced with all the prettiest women in the room.

But the supper dance will be mine, thought Amanda. It would be most singular if he ignored me.

Richard had asked Susan for the supper dance and had been ungraciously accepted. But she *had* accepted, he thought with some amusement. He wondered what Susan would look like with a smile on her face.

A late party of arrivals entered the ballroom, and Richard stiffened and looked wildly around for Amanda. For the girl who had walked into the room was none other than the minx who had made him kiss her in the garden of the seminary.

And she saw him!

Her bold black eyes fastened on him immediately and he could see the smile of recognition on her face.

Anxiously he watched as she and a lady who was undoubtedly her mother stopped to talk to Mrs. Fitzgerald, and then all three started to walk towards him.

Mrs. Fitzgerald performed the introductions. The minx was called Betty Barrington, she whose charms Mrs. Fitzgerald had praised so warmly. Mrs. Fitzgerald and Mrs. Barrington turned to watch the dancers and Betty whispered to Richard, "I knew we should meet again. The next dance is the supper one. You may have it, if you wish."

"That dance is already promised to Miss Fitzgerald," said Richard.

"Then unpromise it," said Betty, "or I shall tell *everyone* that you were asking about the time Lord Hawksborough's carriage would leave on the very day it was robbed by highwaymen!"

Richard's heart gave a lurch, and then he thought he saw a way out.

"You may tell them what you wish," he said lightly, "but I wish you would not, because I am afraid everyone would guess at the real truth."

"You wicked man. What is the real truth? Tell me during supper."

She tugged at his arm, as Susan slouched forward.

"The truth is," said Richard desperately, "that I once saw Susan Fitzgerald by chance and became so enamoured of her, I was determined to find a way to see her again. And, as you can see, I have."

Susan stopped stock-still as if she had been shot and stared at Richard with a dazed look on her face.

"Oh," pouted Betty, hunching a ruffled shoulder. Her quick eyes took in the strained look on Richard's face and the dazed, bewildered look on Susan's, and then she giggled. "I don't believe a word of it. But I shall catch you again!"

She rapped his hand painfully with the sticks of her fan and moved away, still laughing at him over her shoulder.

"My dance, Miss Fitzgerald," said Richard with his best bow. Susan nodded dumbly and moved into his arms. It was the waltz, and Richard had a sudden stab of fright in case he tripped over her feet, his own feet, or anyone else's feet. But the angular set of bones that was Susan Fitzgerald seemed to melt in his arms and it was so easy to spin her around, so fascinating to watch that soft, doubtful look on her normally hard features.

Susan said hardly a word during supper, but Richard had a great deal to talk about, being full of his new life at Oxford, and so he found himself enjoying her undemanding company and felt quite sorry when the time came for them to go back to the ballroom.

As he left the supper room, he saw Amanda, sitting beside a young man. Betty Barrington had stopped to talk to her, and Amanda's startled eyes caught Richard's in a questioning look. He gave a faint shake of the head and smiled to show his unconcern. Somehow, he thought, I must get to Fox End and get the jewels. But how do I get Mr. Cartwright-Browne out of the way while I dig them up?

Amanda was alarmed and worried. Betty had introduced herself and then had said, "Your brother and I have a secret. I met him at Bellingham," and Amanda had immediately known that Betty must be the pert young miss who had sent Richard to fetch the chocolate drops on the day of the highway robbery.

If Lord Hawksborough had partnered her at supper, then Amanda might have had something to take her mind off her fears. But he had chosen to invite an extremely dashing lady of mature years and doubtful morals.

Amanda was overcome by a desire to sulk. But the thought that she was supposed to be in training for that famous husband-catching Season to come made her try to pretend to be happy and flirtatious. She succeeded so well that Lord Hawksborough, watching her flying figure, thought she would be married before the Season even began.

He would have been amazed had he known that Miss Colby was so beset by worries that she could not remember the name of a single partner.

A few gentlemen had discovered that the unprepossessing Susan Fitzgerald danced like an angel. An even greater number became aware of her great dowry—a piece of intelligence which Mrs. Fitzgerald had been quick to spread about the room by dint of forcing Aunt Matilda to gossip for her.

And so, at first amused, and then slightly annoyed, Richard found it increasingly difficult to speak to Miss Fitzgerald, as she was, towards the end of the ball, constantly surrounded by a court of men.

She did not say much, but by dint of appearing to listen intently, she was accounted no end of a fine girl.

Amanda could only be glad when the evening was at last over. Her feet hurt and her head ached.

Lord Hawksborough withdrew to the library, saying he had letters to write as soon as they arrived back in Berkeley Square. He made a formal good-bye to the Colbys. He would be leaving early in the morning. He wished them well.

And that was that.

Amanda sat by the fire in her bedroom, wishing they had never come to London, wishing they had never held up that coach, wishing for her carefree life with Richard to come back again.

She was wearing only her nightgown and wrapper and nightcap and so when the door handle began to turn she called out sharply, "Who is there?" and pulled her wrapper more tightly over her breasts.

The door opened suddenly and Susan Fitzgerald

slouched in. She crashed into an easy chair facing Amanda and scowled at the fire in silence.

"Did you enjoy the ball?" asked Amanda, after she felt she could bear the silence no longer.

"No."

"Well, what *do* you enjoy?" demanded Amanda, wishing Susan would go away.

"All those things my mother calls unmaidenly," said Susan bitterly. "Riding, hunting, fishing."

"Oh, you should have lived with us at Fox End," said Amanda sympathetically. "That was all I *did* do. I did not go to school, I did not have a governess. I had a great deal of household chores, of course, but they did not take the whole of the day."

"Tell me about it," said Susan in her abrupt way.

Amanda began to tell her, diffidently at first and then with greater enthusiasm, about the fun she and Richard had had such a short time ago, "when we were children," Amanda nearly said.

Susan listened avidly, her chin on her hands, her face glowing.

"I should like that above all things," she breathed, when Amanda had finished. "I am not even allowed to gallop in the Park."

Amanda smiled. "Perhaps if I spoke to your mother, she would let us *both* go . . . if I promised we would go early when no one was about."

"Ask her now," said Susan.

"Now? I am in my nightclothes."

"Pooh! Who's to care? The servants are abed. Mama is in her room. Come with me!"

Susan turned and strode from the room. Amanda gave a sigh of exasperation and followed her.

Mrs. Fitzgerald was composing herself for sleep and not at all pleased to be disturbed by Miss Colby demanding that her daughter should be allowed to ride *ventre à terre* through Hyde Park at any hour of the day.

But she ungraciously gave her consent. Her son had told her that very day that he was sure Susan's *farouche* behaviour was the cause of lack of confidence induced by her mother's criticism.

Mrs. Fitzgerald had not believed a word of it, but she was rather in awe of her son, and so she said they might go, provided the hour was early enough and if they were accompanied by two footmen and the head groom.

When they had left her room and shut the door, Susan seized Amanda's hand, gave a gruff thank-you, and fled off down the passageway.

Amanda followed more slowly. Mrs. Fitzgerald had promised the girls would be roused at eight in the morning. It was now, Amanda estimated, about five.

She stopped on the landing of the second floor and leaned over the banister, looking down at the short passage which led to the library on the first.

As she watched, Lord Hawksborough emerged, still in evening dress. She hung tightly onto the wood of the mahogany banister and said a silent farewell.

As if aware of being watched, he looked up. The second-floor landing was in darkness so Amanda was confident that he could not see her, although she could see him, as there was an oil lamp on a chest of drawers on the first landing.

But he said quietly, "Cannot you sleep, Miss Amanda?"

"Susan wanted me to talk to Mrs. Fitzgerald," whispered Amanda.

"Come down," he commanded. "I want to talk to you."

"I am in my undress, my lord."

"Then I am sure you are more clothed than you were in the ballroom. Come down!"

With a fast-beating heart, Amanda scampered down the stairs. He led the way back to the library, where he threw a shovelful of coal on the red embers of the fire and lit one branch of candles on the mantel.

"What did you want to see my mother about?" he asked.

Amanda told him about the early-morning horse-riding project.

"I am glad my mother has agreed," he said testily when she had finished. "But Susan is no longer a baby. She has a tongue in her head. Why the deuce couldn't she ask Mother herself?"

"Perhaps she fears another terrible set-down."

"You make my mother sound like an ogre. Words cannot hurt."

"Yes, they can." Amanda sighed. "They can hurt so terribly and . . . and . . . make one want to do stupid things like taking revenge."

"So wise and yet so young," he mocked. "May I offer you a glass of wine? . . . What is your choice? . . . Madeira? . . . Then I will join you. Sit down, Miss Amanda, and tell me how you enjoyed your first London ball. You were a success, as I was sure you would be."

"You did not ask me to dance," said Amanda, settling herself in the chair by the fire. "You promised you would dance with me."

"Then I will dance with you when I return."

"Will . . . will . . . Mr. Townsend . . . ? I mean, I do not suppose Mr. Townsend will still be pursuing the highwaymen with you gone."

"What put that idea into your pretty head? I sincerely hope he will continue to do the job for which he is being highly paid."

"Oh."

"I suspect you to have a sneaking sympathy for these rogues. You read too many romances, Miss Amanda. Do you know that every time you talk about that robbery, your eyes take on a hunted look. One would think you a highway robber yourself!"

"You did not answer my question," said Amanda quickly, desperate to change the subject.

"Which one?"

"Why did you not dance with me?"

"Perhaps I forgot."

"Perhaps," echoed Amanda in a small voice.

"I will be honest with you," he said quietly. "It may sound very vain, but I was afraid you might have formed a *tendre* for me." She gave a soft exclamation and he held up his hand. "No, let me go on. I am very much older than you, my child. I am thirty. Sometimes when one is as young as you, one forms a *tendre* for someone older. That someone is never the person that one would love in later years."

"How do you know?" asked Amanda, the lace at the bosom of her nightdress revealed by the open wrapper rising and falling.

"I am engaged to be married."

"You have begged my question. And that was the only reason you did not ask me to dance?"

"Not quite. I find you—"

But before he could finish what he was about to say, a great gust of wind tore at the windows and the candles blew out. He gave an exclamation of impatience. "I will close the shutters if you will relight the candles."

He strode to the window. Amanda put a taper between the bars of the fire and then stretched on tiptoe to try to light the candles on the mantelshelf. But they were too high, so after a little deliberation she climbed up on her chair and then stood on the arm, and lit the candles one by one. He was returning and she was stretching out to reach the last candle when the chair she was standing on wobbled dangerously.

"Silly child," said Lord Hawksborough. "You will end up in the fire."

He caught her in his arms and swung her down onto the rug in front of the fire. He had meant to release her immediately, but even through his waistcoat he could feel her small high breasts pressing against him. He was conscious of a faint scent of roses from her hair, of the pliant softness of her body, of the drowned lost look in those strange green-gold eyes turned up to his own.

Then she veiled her eyes with her lashes and turned her mouth a fraction up towards him and gave a little sigh of submission.

He felt his pulses racing and a constriction in his chest, and he suddenly, cruelly wanted to know if he could shock her senses more than she had shocked his. It was unbelievable that such a little slip of a girl could rouse such violent feelings in him.

He put his hand under her chin and lightly brushed her mouth with his own. Then he kissed a little blue vein at the base of her left ear, and brought his other hand up to tangle in the masses of curly soft hair, brushed free from its fashionable coiffure.

Her whole body seemed to throb and vibrate in his arms, and he thought wryly that he would give her one good kiss on the mouth to punish her, and then send her off to bed.

But as his mouth closed over her own, her lips, soft and warm, opened instinctively under his, and somehow the next moment he was sitting in the armchair with her on his lap, while each movement of his busy hands and busy mouth seemed to drive them both mad.

To Amanda, it was as if they were both whirling through space and time, fused together by passion. He kissed her for a long time, his senses assaulted by hair and perfume of roses, and lips and arms, and candlelight and firelight, and the glitter and desire in those thick-fringed green-and-gold eyes.

Outside, the mounting storm tore at the building and howled in the chimneys.

His exploring hand slid inside the neck of her nightgown and closed around one small perfect breast.

Amanda's body went very still and her lips beneath his own stopped moving.

The room swung back into focus.

Lord Hawksborough gave a ragged sigh and realised in dawning horror that he had been within an ames-ace of seducing his mother's young guest.

"You witch!" he said suddenly and savagely, and pushed her off his lap. Amanda regained her balance and stood up. Her eyes were wide and dark and her mouth was swollen and bruised.

"My dear Amanda," he said, obviously fighting for control. "You asked me why I did not ask you to dance. That is your answer. I knew I could not trust myself if I held you in my arms."

"Then?" said Amanda, taking a step towards him as he stood up. "Then . . .?"

"It's madness. I am engaged. The whole thing is folly and madness. *No!* Don't dare come near me. I must confess I drank overmuch tonight. I am not myself. Do not look at me so. Be the good child you are and run along to bed. I will be gone by the time you wake, and when I return, you will be engaged to a suitable young man. Please do not distress me further nor make me more ashamed of what I have done. I beg of you. Leave me."

Amanda looked sadly and searchingly up into his face, but his mouth was set and his eyes were cold, and he brushed himself down and straightened his waistcoat with a certain fastidious distaste which cut her to the quick.

All at once she ran from the room and slammed the door behind her.

He stood for a long time looking into the embers of the fire, his face as grim and hard as it had been when Amanda had first seen him at the assembly at Hember Cross.

6

Amanda was awakened almost, it seemed, five minutes after she had dropped off to sleep. She heard the wind still roaring outside, but knew that Susan would be hell-bent on riding, no matter what the weather.

It proved to be as good a tonic as any for a sore heart. The two girls galloped side by side through the empty Park, Amanda on a borrowed horse and Susan on her black horse called Pericles. At last, even Susan felt she had had enough exercise and shouted above the wind that they should return home.

They swung their mounts around and cantered side by side under the tossing trees. Amanda was wearing a wool dress and cloak but Susan was wearing a dashing riding habit of bright green cloth, ornamented down the front and on the cuffs *à la militaire* with black braid.

They were nearing the gates of the Park when they saw an odd figure approaching.

A great rawboned horse was bearing a slim masculine figure dressed in dandified morning dress. His guinea-gold curls peeped out from beneath a wide-awake, and as he came nearer, the girls were able to see he had a very beautiful, sensitive face and vague blue eyes.

He reined in his horse and Susan and Amanda brought their mounts to a halt. He made a low bow which nearly sent him flying over his horse's ears, looked at Susan and put his hand on his heart and sighed, and then with another low bow he pressed the heels of his spurless hessians into his horse's flanks and moved on.

"What a court card!" said Susan, urging her horse forward again.

"He seemed much taken with you, Susan." Amanda giggled.

"Yes," said Susan smugly. "It is amazing to find that I am attractive after all."

Amanda cast her a doubtful glance but reflected charitably that Susan could do with a little vanity.

They were ambling through Grosvenor Square on their way to Berkeley Square when a light travelling carriage rounded the square pulled by four horses. Seated on the box was Lord Hawksborough. He raised his whip in salute but did not stop. Amanda watched him go, her heart in her eyes and resentment in her heart.

He had casually made her aware that she was now a woman with all a woman's passions. But he had called her a child, and he had not even stayed his horses to say good-bye.

She was glad to be able to leave Susan as soon as they returned home and fall into bed again.

That evening, Mrs. Fitzgerald was entertaining in style. She held a dinner party for twenty. Susan appeared *en grande tenue* and adopted the airs of a reigning beauty. Amanda blushed for her, until she realised that

Susan was well on the way to becoming the latest fashion.

Gossip was about the victory celebration of the previous June and the eccentricities of the visiting royals. The Emperor of Russia and the King of Prussia had not given any money to the state coachmen and cooks. The King of Prussia had eaten voraciously at half-past two each day, and one day eleven loins of veal were cut up for his hundred and eighty attendants. The Emperor, for three months' stay at the Pulteney, had only given two hundred pounds amongst thirty servants. And so the gossip went.

Amanda listened intently to every word until she realised she was saving every *on-dit*, dreaming of sitting in the library telling every bit of it to Lord Hawksborough on his return. But he would not want to see *her* on his return, she thought miserably. He would no doubt pat her on the head and give her sugar plums and rush off to the well-rounded arms of Lady Mary Dane.

That evening party was the start of many. Aunt Matilda became more and more animated as the pressure of social engagements grew.

Mrs. Fitzgerald now praised her daughter's appearance lavishly, and Susan, from being a sulky gauche girl, became a swollen-headed gauche girl, and then gradually began to settle down and acquire a dignified air of breeding and a quieter, easier manner. The beautiful young man who had been so enraptured with Susan that day in the Park had managed to introduce himself to Mrs. Fitzgerald and was a constant visitor. His name was Mr. Bertram Dalzell, a young man of good family. He kept sending Susan long poems which she would read aloud to Amanda, punctuating the lines with gurgles of laughter.

Christmas was celebrated in the Hanoverian manner with a tree at one end of the room and presents piled on a table at the other.

Amanda had saved most of her allowance so that she could repay a little of her hostess's generosity by buying Mrs. Fitzgerald a cashmere shawl.

Young men came and young men went and Amanda paid not the slightest heed to any of them. Despite the fact that her mind was telling her that Lord Hawksborough was engaged to be married and that he thought of her as a child, she knew she was waiting, waiting, counting the days until his return.

Lady Mary came back to London one snowy day, dropping from her reticule, by deliberate accident, a bunch of love letters tied up with pink ribbon. She snatched them up and gave a rueful laugh, her clear blue gaze going to where Amanda sat sewing in a corner of the Red Drawing Room. "Charles's letters," she said with a shrug. "He is such a passionate man, Mrs. Fitzgerald. I would be put to the blush if anyone saw even one line!"

Amanda lowered her eyes to her sewing, but her thoughts were racing.

Lord Hawksborough was right, she thought grimly. She *was* a schoolgirl. Only a schoolgirl would sit pining away for an unattainable man who had no interest in her whatsoever, a man who wrote passionate letters to his fiancée.

She, Amanda, would have to leave London after the Season was over. The Season began in May and finished in July. And then what?

I must make a push to secure a husband, thought Amanda fiercely. Richard's studies have only just begun. 'Twould be no hardship to be married to someone comfortable—an elderly gentleman, say, who only wishes a companion.

Her determination was further cemented a few days later when she received a letter from Richard. He had reclaimed the jewels and burned the masks and wigs and hats. He had stayed at Bellingham, being frightened to show his face at Hember Cross. He had learned Mr. Cartwright-Browne had found Mr. Brotherington snooping around the garden of Fox End and was charging him with trespass. On the day of the court hearing, Richard had gone to Fox End and had affected to be surprised to find the master not at home. He had told Mr. Cartwright-Browne's butler that he would like to see his horse, Caesar.

Once in the stable, he had locked the doors and unearthed the jewels. He would return to London during the small hours of Sunday morning.

Amanda was to creep down the stairs and unbar the door. They would leave the jewel box in the hall.

Amanda gave a sigh of relief. She sat down with the letter crushed in her hand, her legs trembling. All at once she realized she had been living all the time since her arrival in London in great fear of being found out. Now the nightmare was over.

Life had become ordinary. She was used to London society. She must grow up and find herself a husband and then remove herself as far away from Lord Hawksborough's unsettling personality as possible.

On Saturday, they were to see Kean perform in

Othello, so Amanda was confident of being back in Berkeley Square well before two o'clock in the morning.

The party for the theater was made up of Mrs. Fitzgerald; Aunt Matilda; Lady Mary; Susan Fitzgerald; Amanda; the beautiful Mr. Dalzell, who was being encouraged in his attentions to Susan by Mrs. Fitzgerald, who had found out that the young man had a not inconsiderable fortune; Lord Box, an elderly friend of Mrs. Fitzgerald's; Colonel John Withers of the Hussars, a ferocious military gentleman who seemed quite dazzled by Lady Mary; and Mr. Tom Moore, the poet.

The performance absorbed Amanda's attention completely. Kean's acting was superb.

And when the performance was over and Mr. Moore offered to escort them to the green room to meet the great man, Amanda was so excited at the thought of meeting the actor that she forgot about the jewel box and the time.

The green room was a small apartment with a large looking glass and a sofa all around it—yellow, not green.

Mr. Kean at last made his offstage entrance. He was a very short man, wearing a pepper-and-salt suit. But he was strongly made and wide-shouldered, with a hollow, sallow face and thick black hair. Mr. Moore asked after his health and he replied mildly that it was tolerable but that he was having trouble with his voice.

Amanda had heard reports of the actor's amusing stories, but he seemed tired that night, and uncomfortable in the presence of so many strangers.

Miss Smith, who had played Desdemona, came in, and Mrs. Fitzgerald remarked loudly that she bore a marked resemblance to Lady Tavistock—a middle-aged peeress famous for the amount of paint with which she bedaubed her face and bosom—and Susan cackled with laughter.

Mr. Moore winced and brought the audience to an end. Not for the first time did Amanda wonder how Lord Hawksborough had managed to acquire such charm and ease of manner. Not from his mother anyway.

Then she remembered Richard and the jewels, and was all at once in a fever to be gone.

The wait for the carriages seemed endless; then there was chitchat over the tea tray at Berkeley Square for what seemed hours, although it was only half an hour, and at last everyone, with the exception of that almost permanent houseguest, Lady Mary, left.

Amanda sat on the edge of her bed, watching the little gilt clock on the mantel, her heart thudding so loudly that it seemed to drown out the chattering tick-tock of the clock.

The time was one-thirty. How slowly the hands moved at first! And how fast they began to race as two o'clock neared!

She crept very quietly down the stairs, still wearing the blue silk gown she had worn to the theater—a Christmas present from Mrs. Fitzgerald.

The long train of the dress made a soft shur-shurring sound on the stairs and she impatiently caught it up and carried it over her arm.

Very quietly she unbarred the door and then turned the great key in the lock.

The grandfather clock behind her gave a loud whir preparatory to striking the hour and she nearly jumped out of her skin with fright.

A fire was burning in the hall and the flames sent

their shadows dancing up the walls. In every moving shadow she thought she saw the heavy, bulky figure of the thief-taker.

And then the door began to open.

"Richard," hissed Amanda as he cautiously put his head around the door. "Oh, Richard! I thought you would never come!" And great tears of relief began to roll down her face.

"Stop blubbing," he said sharply, "and help me with the curst box."

It was a small square black iron box with a handle at either end. Amanda seized one handle and Richard took the other. They lowered the box gently to the floor.

"I've got a note," said Richard. "I scribbled it to make it look as if it had been written by a semiliterate person."

"What did you say?"

"Only 'Here's the jewels. We're sorry.' "

"Can you stay?"

"Of course I can't, stoopid. How is Susan?"

"Very well. She is quite the fashion."

"*Susan!*"

"Yes, Susan. And she has become amazing vain."

"Now, Amanda, you're jealous."

"I am not jealous!"

"Who's there!" cried a voice from upstairs.

Amanda and Richard clutched each other in fright.

"Quickly! Go!" said Amanda.

"No. Whoever it is might give chase, and I'll be caught by the watch," hissed Richard. "Hide! Over here!"

They crept quietly into a corner of the hall, far away

from the dancing light of the fire, and hid behind the massive grandfather clock.

They heard the soft swish of silk, and then a man's voice calling again. "Who's below?"

Silence.

Richard looked around the corner of the clock and gave a muttered exclamation of dismay. Amanda put her hand softly over his mouth and then asked softly, "Who is it?"

"Hawksborough," said Richard in a faint whisper.

Steps could be heard descending the stairs. Holding a candle, Lord Hawksborough walked across the hall to the door. He was wearing a magnificent peacock-blue silk dressing gown with gold frogs.

He almost stumbled over the box. He stopped and looked down. Slowly he stooped and picked up the letter which was lying on top of the box and quickly scanned the contents. His face looked hard and grim.

He picked up the box and tucked it under one arm. Then he raised his candle high and his eyes raked around the hall.

Then he crossed quickly to the wall opposite from where Richard and Amanda were standing and pulled savagely on the bell rope.

Richard felt behind him with his hand and found the door to the Red Drawing Room. He opened the door and gently eased himself and Amanda inside and thankfully closed the door.

They stayed close together, pressing their ears to the panels of the door, hearing the sleepy, protesting voice of the butler saying that the outside door had been barred because he had seen to it himself.

More servants were called, and more questions.

What if they search the house! thought Amanda wildly. How could she explain Richard's presence?

At last there was the sound of the door being barred and locked again.

More voices, and then silence.

Still they waited. "Half-past two and a starry night. All's well!" called the gloomy voice of the watch from the square.

Only half an hour, thought Amanda. I feel as if we have been waiting here a lifetime.

They waited and waited until at last they heard the watch cry the three o'clock. Both of them were stiff with cold and tension.

"Now!" said Richard.

He gently eased open the door of the Red Drawing Room and they slipped into the hall.

The fire had died down and the hall was shrouded in a welcome blackness.

Taking infinite pains not to make the slightest noise, Richard unbarred the door. He gave Amanda a quick hug, and vanished as silently as a shadow out into the street.

Forcing herself not to rush, Amanda lowered the bars over the door and softly turned the key again, and locked it.

It took a tremendous effort not to make a blind headlong dash for the stairs.

She moved slowly and carefully, putting one foot in front of the other, holding her train over her arm.

She passed the oil lamp's light of the first landing, and thankfully ascended up into the darkness of the second flight of stairs.

A sound below made her swing around, and for one

split second she saw Lord Hawksborough, and immediately turned fully around as if she were descending the stairs. And not a moment too soon. For he held up his candle so that the ring of light caught the hem of her dress.

"It's Amanda, isn't it?" he said. "What are you doing out of bed?"

"Welcome home, my lord," said Amanda, coming down the stairs, amazed to find her own voice sounding so calm. "I could not sleep and thought I heard a noise and came to investigate."

"It is obvious you could not sleep," he said, looking her up and down. "You are still fully dressed. You may as well come and talk to me." He turned and led the way to the library.

Amanda knew that she should plead fatigue, in case something in her face gave her away. And she did not mean to betray her knowledge of the theft of the jewels. She was frightened he would read in her eyes her overwhelming happiness that he was home again. But he drew her like a magnet.

He lit the candle in the library and turned and looked at her again. For a long moment they studied each other. He was wearing a thin cambric nightshirt under his dressing gown and his black hair was tousled as if he had run his fingers through it. His bare feet were thrust into red morocco slippers.

Lord Hawksborough thought Amanda had changed. The blue gown was cut low to reveal the top halves of her two excellent white breasts. Her hair had been curled and arranged in a Grecian style for the play, but now it was reverting to its usual cloud of curls which framed her piquant face and elfin eyes.

He felt something tug at his heart and quickly told her about finding the jewels.

To his surprise, she did not exclaim or look startled, merely said in a matter-of-fact way, "Well, Mr. Townsend will be glad to stop his search."

"Why should he do that?" asked Lord Hawksborough. "Do not stand over by the door, Amanda. Come and sit by the fire. I have no intention of calling off Mr. Townsend. I want these thieves arrested."

"But why?" asked Amanda, moving quickly to the seat by the fire and averting her face from his so that he might not see her distress. "You have the jewels."

"My dear Amanda, I have the jewels, as you point out. I also have my pride. One of these ruffians had the temerity to rob me from the back of a donkey. A donkey! And the other deliberately set out to humiliate me by taking my ring. That ring, my dear Amanda, was a personal present from the Prince Regent when I was awarded my viscountcy."

"But—"

"I weary of this perpetual topic of the highwaymen. Forget them. It is a job for the law. Now, tell me how you have been getting on."

He sat down opposite her, and the warmth in his eyes made Amanda want to cry.

He had no right to walk back into her life and casually pick up her heart and wrench it like a spoiled child mangling a cast-off toy.

"When did you get back?" she asked.

"This evening. While you were at the play. I was tired and went straight to bed. Something awoke me. I thought I heard a faint sound from below. But that brings us back to the jewels." He moved to pour her a glass of wine and the great ruby ring once more blazed on his hand. "Tell me how you go on," he insisted. "Have you a beau?"

"Not yet." Amanda smiled. "It is Susan who is become the *succès fou* of society. She is become the fashion."

"I hope it does not go to her head. Eccentrics are often fêted out of Season and totally ignored in it. Or has her manner changed?"

"I don't know. Yes . . . it has changed . . ."

"But not for the better?"

"I did not say that."

"But your eyes did. Also that quick nervous turn of your head. *You* have changed. You are become a woman, Amanda."

His eyes rested fleetingly on her bosom and returned to her face.

"And you," said Amanda. "Was your business successful?"

"I achieved what I set out to achieve, in one way. In the other, no, I think I have failed to convince my masters of the seriousness of the situation."

"Can you tell me about it?"

"Perhaps. A little. You must not tell anyone. Even Richard."

"I will not tell."

He studied her in silence and then settled back in his chair.

"I shall tell you," he said at last. "I went to meet a piece of history, but I fear that piece of history is shortly going to create future trouble."

"You speak in riddles."

"I shall begin at the beginning. I went to see Napoleon."

"That monster! But he is in prison, is he not?"

"He rides about the island of Elba like a lord on his country estate. I set about getting an audience with him. This I did by positioning myself beside the road from Porto Ferrajo and waiting until he came riding past. I pulled off my hat and made him a low bow. Napoleon stopped with Drouot, who was riding with him, and asked, *"Qui êtes-vous?"* I am sorry, Amanda. Do you understand French?"

"Only a little."

"Very well. He said, 'Who are you?' and I replied, 'An Englishman.' He asked, 'Are you a soldier?' I shook my head. 'Shopkeeper?' I shook my head again. *'Alors*, you are a gentleman,' he said. 'Come with me.'

"He said he was going to his country house in San Martino and we would talk there. Once we arrived at San Martino, Napoleon took me into a small room and shut the door.

"He seemed used to being treated like a sort of curiosity and said I could ask him any questions I liked.

"I asked him the first one that came to mind. I asked, 'Why did you stay so long at Moscow? That was the beginning of your downfall.'

"He replied, 'I looked over the meteorological tables for the last thirty years, and never but once had the winter set in so early, by five weeks, as it did in 1812. I could not foresee that. I made mistakes, as every man does, in the many years that I have been in public life and a soldier—perhaps ten a day.'

"Napoleon went on to say that he thought Wellington was a brave man. He said he would sooner trust him with one hundred thousand men than any of his generals, even Soult. He often laughed violently, great bursts of laughter, and he flew from one topic to the next. He asked me what I thought of the Princess Charlotte and whether she was not a person of spirit and character. The next minute he raged about reports that when he was at council he used to cut the chairs and even the throne with his penknife.

"I asked him if he were afraid of assassination. 'Not by the English,' he replied. 'Perhaps by the Corsicans. They do not love me.'

"I perhaps should have assassinated him myself," said Lord Hawksborough, pouring more wine for himself and Amanda.

"But why?"

"Listen! I asked the all-important question. I asked if he had any ambitions to return to French soil and be restored to his former glory. He shrugged and said, *Mon rôle est fini.*' He said he was writing his history. 'Napoleon is always Napoleon,' he said, 'and always will know how to be content to bear any fortune.'

"But as I took my leave of him, he said again, *'Mon rôle est fini,'* my role is finished, but he followed it up with a great burst of laughter which had a mocking edge. The island was alive with rumours of his planned escape.

"And so I returned to London and advised my masters that the Emperor should be moved forthwith to a more secure place of confinement. But they shrugged and thanked me for my services and said I would be suitably rewarded, but that there was no danger in the world of Napoleon ever escaping from Elba."

Lord Hawksborough stretched and yawned. "I am devilish tired, Amanda."

"Then come to bed!" laughed a voice from the doorway.

Lady Mary stood watching them with a warm smile on her lips which did not meet her eyes. She was wearing a white peignoir of pink cashmere with a Persian border.

"How long have you been there listening?" demanded Lord Hawksborough.

"I did not listen at all," protested Lady Mary. "My dear Charles, such a welcome!"

He walked forward and raised her hand and kissed it. She wound her arms about him and leaned back and looked at him through half-closed lids. "Well, Charles, are you not glad to see me?"

Lord Hawksborough put his arms about her, but he turned his head slightly towards where Amanda was now standing.

"Miss Colby," said Lady Mary in a caressing voice. "Do you not feel you are somewhat *de trop?*"

"I was just going," said Amanda, blushing to the roots of her hair. She ran from the room and up the stairs to her bedroom, where she hurled herself face-down on the bed and bit the counterpane in an access of pain and mortification. How could he embrace Lady Mary so? The library was where she, Amanda, talked to him.

"But they were not talking when you left, nor interested in talking," prompted her inner voice.

Amanda had just made up her mind to have a really good sort of wallowing bout of tears when she became aware that someone was throwing pebbles at her window.

She knew that sound of old, because Richard used to throw pebbles at her bedroom window at Fox End when he returned from one of his late-night fishing expeditions.

She lifted the sash of the window and looked down into the square.

It was indeed Richard standing under the parish lamp.

"You'll need to let me in," he said in a faint whisper. "I haven't enough money to pay my shot at an inn."

"Hammer on the knocker and tell them you are just arrived," hissed Amanda.

"Daren't! Too risky. Might think it a coincidence. Oxford stage got in hours ago. Frightened they connect me with the jewels."

"Oh, very well," said Amanda, although she thought he was being ridiculous. Any servant would assume he had been out drinking with friends. Then she thought crossly that they should both have thought of that in the first place instead of all this havey-cavey business. Richard should simply have arrived with the jewels hidden in his luggage.

She ran downstairs again, this time unafraid she would be heard. She unbarred and unlocked the door.

Richard followed her silently upstairs and Amanda held her tongue until they were both locked in her bedroom.

"This secrecy is silly, Richard," she said. "You could simply have walked through the front door."

"I suppose so," said Richard. "But I am afraid that we will still be found out. Let us hope Townsend has been called off."

"He hasn't," replied Amanda. "My lord told me this

evening that he still wants the highwaymen brought to justice."

"I can't be found here," said Richard, looking about wildly. "He'll think it monstrous strange if I turn up the same night as the jewels."

"Perhaps," sighed Amanda, suddenly very tired. "Go and sleep on the chaise longue, Richard, at the foot of the bed, and I will awaken you early and give you money for the stage. I am sure it is all unnecessary—the secrecy, that is—but I am too fatigued to think."

"Very well"—Richard yawned—"but I must say Hawksborough is an amazingly tenacious man. Anyone else would simply have been glad to get the jewels back."

Lord Hawksborough led Lady Mary gently away from outside Amanda's bedroom door.

He had been leading her along to her own room to say good night to her, and had been busy examining his strange new feelings of distaste towards his fiancée when she had stopped outside Amanda's door and whispered to him to listen.

Faintly through the thick panels came the sound of a man's voice.

"Aren't you going in?" demanded Lady Mary. "She has a man in her room!"

Lord Hawksborough urged her down the corridor. "Well," she demanded, "what do you think of your Miss Prunes and Prisms now?"

"I am very tired," he said quietly. "I will talk to Amanda in the morning. Good night, Mary."

She gave him a baffled look, but he was already turning away, and he had not kissed her good night.

Lord Hawksborough walked back to Amanda's room and tried the door.

Locked.

He was assailed with such a wave of jealous fury that he thought he would die. Amanda Colby was no innocent. His strange passion for her was because she obviously knew to a nicety how to fuel it.

What a fool he had been.

He would deal with her in the morning. It *was* morning, dammit. He looked at the clock. Six! He set his mind to wake at nine and at last lay down on his bed and tried to compose his mind for sleep. But he was overtired—too overtired to sleep, and the rage would not leave him. A sane corner of his mind was telling him he was being ridiculous to become so exercised over a young girl when he was already engaged. But his emotions cried that somehow she had deceived him with her air of innocence. That she had made a fool of him, by God!

And so it was at *eight* in the morning that Amanda awoke to a summons from a footman outside her door. His lordship wished to see her *immediately*.

Without waking Richard, Amanda splashed water on her face and scrambled into her clothes. She brushed her hair furiously and then tried to braid it, but her fingers could not seem to manage to get it under control, and so she compromised by twisting her hair into a hard knot on the top of her head. Wearing a dull blue kerseymere gown—a new addition to her wardrobe—she ran down the stairs. The servant had not said where Lord Hawksborough was to be found. He was not in the library.

By dint of asking various servants who were going

about their duties, she was startled to learn that his lordship was in his bedchamber.

Feeling very nervous, she followed the magnificent livery of one of the footmen elected to guide her. She did not think for a moment that Lord Hawksborough wished to see her for any mild conversation at this unearthly hour of the morning.

At Fox End, Amanda would have already been up and about two hours ago, but she had become accustomed to London hours and knew hardly anyone ever arose before noon.

Lord Hawksborough was invisible behind a cloud of lather when she entered, and his valet was stooped over him with a razor. Amanda made to withdraw, but Lord Hawksborough waved her into a seat at the other side of the room.

Amanda sat down primly and waited with a beating heart. It could not be the jewels. He would not have troubled to let himself be barbered were that the case. Amanda felt sure he would have come to her bedroom and broken down the door had he found out.

At last his lordship was shaved and the valet dismissed.

He stood up, still in his dressing gown, and looked her up and down with hard, assessing eyes. "Amazing!" he remarked.

"My lord?"

"Come here!"

He had a devilish glint in his eyes, but Amanda reminded herself that he was her host and that she had nothing to be afraid of—provided he had not found out about the robbery.

She walked towards him and stood meekly, her hands behind her back, her eyes downcast.

"Now we shall see," he said half to himself.

He picked her up and tossed her on the bed and threw himself on top of her.

"Charles!" screamed Amanda, her eyes wide with shock.

"It's no use screaming," he said grimly. "My servants are too well-trained to interfere in my pleasures."

His mouth clamped down on hers, and Amanda was swept with a mixture of passion and sheer fright.

It was only when he raised his head and ripped open the front of her dress with one savage wrench of his hand, and she saw the blind mask of anger that was his face, that all passion fled and sheer instinct for survival took over.

"Charles!" she screamed in horror. "You are trying to rape me!"

"Not rape . . . take," he said, one hand clipping her hands behind her back and his mouth sinking down to kiss her left breast.

Shocked, stunned, and bitterly disappointed in him, Amanda began to cry. Great tears rolled down her face and she sobbed and gulped.

He rolled off her immediately and sat up.

"I think Kean has a rival," he said coldly.

"I don't *understand*!" wailed Amanda.

"Don't play the innocent virgin with me, Amanda," he said harshly. "I find I have not the stomach to take you after all. But do not insult me or my mother by harbouring lovers in your bedchamber. Who is he?"

"Who . . . ? Richard! It is Richard!"

"Stuff!"

"It *is*," said Amanda, wriggling away to the other side of the bed. "I let him in last night. He had come to town to spend a few hours drinking with friends and had not the money for a hotel. He threw pebbles at my window after I had left you with Lady Mary. I let him in."

"Take me to him!" he barked.

Amanda looked down at her ripped gown in despair.

He followed her glance, and, with an impatient exclamation, strode to the wardrobe and pulled out another dressing gown. "Here, put this on," he said, throwing it at her.

Amanda wrapped herself in the dressing gown and tied the sash about her small waist and held the fold of the material tight about her throat. It was too big for her, and folds of it trailed about her feet.

Richard sat up with a groan as they entered the room. "I had best be leaving." He yawned.

Then he caught sight of Lord Hawksborough and flushed to the roots of his hair.

"If you are making your way back to Oxford to continue your studies, Colby," said the viscount in measured tones, "then I suggest you do so. In future, should you decide to honor us with your presence, then may I suggest you use the room allotted to you."

"I did not want to disturb the servants—" began Richard.

"I pay my servants very good wages," said Lord Hawksborough. "It is their job to be disturbed. If you will now go to your own bedroom, I will send my valet to assist you in your toilet."

He stood aside and held open the door while Richard, who had slept in his clothes, scrambled to his feet. Then Richard noticed Amanda wrapped in the folds of a man's dressing gown, and his eyes grew wide.

"I spilled coffee on my gown," said Amanda hurriedly. "His lordship sent for me because a man's voice was heard coming from my bedroom and everyone imagined the worst. Please *go*, Richard!"

Richard left the room, glad to get away from his lordship's angry face.

Lord Hawksborough slammed the door behind him and turned to Amanda. "I offer you my apologies, Amanda," he said. "I have behaved disgracefully. You may be sure I shall not touch you again. There is something between us which should not exist. It would be better if we avoided each other's company in the future."

"But—" began Amanda dismally.

"I cannot remember having behaved so badly in the whole of my life," he said savagely. "You're a Circe, Amanda!"

Amanda began to feel guilty. The guilt was irrational, she knew, but like most guilty people, she started working herself up into a rage.

"This *thing* that you say is between us, my lord," she said angrily, "is perhaps, merely a figment of your imagination. I was naturally overwhelmed at receiving an excess of civility from a peer in your position. I am not yet used to the ways of gentlemen, or to the ways of the world."

"Obviously," he said coldly. "Or you would not accept an apology with such bad grace."

"I was under the impression I had not accepted it at all," flashed Amanda.

"I have no intention wasting more time bandying vulgar words with you," he said with great hauteur. "I am very tired. Good day to you, ma'am."

He gathered the folds of his dressing gown about him and strode to the door.

The bottle of Otto of Roses which Amanda had seized and thrown in a blind rage smashed against the doorjamb inches from his face.

The whole room was permeated by the heavy smell of roses.

He turned around, not just his head, but all in one piece.

"I am sorry," babbled Amanda.

He turned again like a clockwork toy and walked out into the passageway.

Amanda ran after him and caught his sleeve. "Charles!" she pleaded. "You must realise how very angry you can make me."

He tugged his sleeve to get it free, and only succeeded in pulling her against him.

"I think . . . yes, I really think I am going to demand an explanation," came the silky voice of Lady Mary.

Her blue eyes took in the scene. Lord Hawksborough and Amanda, both wearing dressing gowns, were standing close together. Amanda looked dishevelled and her lips were swollen. The whole passageway stank of Otto of Roses.

The silence seemed to stretch forever. "The first time I met this little girl," went on Lady Mary, her fine eyes going from one to the other, "she smelled like a Covent Garden brothel. I recall wondering if this were one of your *traviatas*, Charles."

Amanda, despite her distress, vividly remembered spilling the perfume over her arm on her first evening in London.

"Come with me, Lady Mary," said Lord Hawksborough heavily. "It is not what you think."

Lady Mary raked Amanda up and down with a contemptuous glance, and edged her way past, drawing her skirts about her as if the very touch of Amanda's hem would contaminate her.

Amanda sighed and went back into her room and shut the door. She was bone-tired. She slumped into a chair and stared vacantly into space.

At last she roused herself from her numbed state to turn the problem of Lord Hawksborough over in her mind. She did not love him. He roused her senses, that was all. It was surely nothing more than rampant lust. He had not behaved at all like a man in love, thought Amanda, whose ideas of how men in love behaved were still well-grounded in the gothic novels she had read.

There had never been the slightest hint of a worshipful expression in his lordship's eyes. He had untrustworthy eyes, those strange silver eyes which were so good at masking his feelings.

She must struggle out of this infatuation and concentrate on saving the family fortunes. Her mind turned to the elderly Lord Box, who had accompanied them to the play. He had been quiet and courteous and kind. He had laughed in a shy way at her mildest witticisms. He was said to be a widower and vastly rich.

The idea of marriage to Lord Box began to seem attractive to Amanda, particularly when it was followed with a pleasing dream of breaking the news of her engagement to Lord Hawksborough.

Having come to some sort of decision, Amanda decided to go to bed.

But the door burst open and Susan marched in and

crashed down into a chair beside the fire and stared moodily at the flames. "Rot!" she said at last.

"Rot what?" asked Amanda, wishing she would go away. Her head was beginning to ache with stress and lack of sleep.

"Dalzell is on the point of proposing to me. I asked Lady Mary for her advice, because I think she is a very *mondaine* lady, and she said, 'You had better snap him up.' 'Why?' says I. 'I am accounted attractive by more gentlemen than Dalzell, and Dalzell is a milksop.' And she says, 'You are an Original, dear Susan, and Originals quickly grow unfashionable. You are well enough in your way, but you have hardly got the sort of face that would launch a thousand ships. Perhaps a small coal barge.' "

"How malicious, and how untrue," said Amanda warmly.

"But Lady Mary is so sensible. It was she who spoke to Mama on my behalf and told Mama to stop criticising my appearance."

"Indeed! I was under the impression that suggestion came from your brother."

"Charles? Charles would not trouble with me."

"On the contrary, he is very concerned about you."

"How do *you* know?" said Susan rudely. "And what are you doing wearing one of Charles's dressing gowns?"

Wearily Amanda altered and retold the lie of the spilled coffee.

"Well, in any case, what am I to do about Mr. Dalzell?"

"Do you have *anything* in common?" asked Amanda.

"No. I tried to talk hunting with him, and all it elicited was a poem. It goes, 'Diana, like the moon above . . .' although why on earth he should call me Diana when my name is Susan, I'll never know.

> " 'Diana, like the moon above,
>   Silent, chaste, serene
>   Mistress of the hunter's love
>   In the woodland green. . . .'

"Pah!"

"Then it is all very simple," said Amanda, stifling a yawn. "You hold him in contempt. Above all, you are not in love with him——"

"Love? When did love ever get in the way of a society marriage?" said Susan crossly.

"I'm tired, very tired," said Amanda, putting her hands to her throbbing temples. "I shall see you later, Susan."

"But what shall I do about Mr. Dalzell?"

"A very kind thing to do would be to make it plain to him that you would not favour his suit. 'Twould be very cruel to encourage him only to repulse him. I gather that London is still thin of company, but there will be plenty of unattached gentlemen during the Season who will share your country interests. You are an attractive girl, Susan, when you are not scowling and angry. Besides, you listen so intently to everything a gentlemen says to you, and *that* seems to be more seductive than any beauty."

"All right," said Susan, getting awkwardly to her feet.

She suddenly smiled down at Amanda, a smile so sweet and blinding, so like her brother's, that Amanda's heart gave a painful wrench. "I like you," said Susan. "You're a great gun."

She bent and kissed Amanda on the cheek and then cheerfully clumped from the room, slamming the door behind her so that the very furniture seemed to shudder.

"Well," said Amanda Colby, putting her hand up to her cheek. "Well, well, well . . . and I thought she was not like her brother at all."

And then Amanda reminded herself that thinking about Lord Hawksborough's smile was certainly not going to help her forget him.

But she wrapped his dressing gown tightly about her and fell asleep, facedown on the bed, her hand buried among its silken folds, still holding it across her breast.

7

Whatever Lord Hawksborough had said to his fiancée by way of explanation seemed to have banished her anger and fear. Once more Lady Mary was glowing. Once more she was forever by his side.

Nonetheless, she often watched Amanda when she thought the girl wasn't looking, watching to see if Miss Colby showed any signs of warmth towards Lord Hawksborough. But it appeared that, for Amanda, Lord Hawksborough had ceased to exist.

She was busy encouraging the attentions of Lord Box.

Amanda found Lord Box very soothing. He took her driving in the Park, he escorted her to the opera, always including Aunt Matilda in his invitations.

He was a small dapper man, not overly wrinkled considering his fifty-five years. He wore his hair powdered, despite the iniquitous flour tax, and was always formally, if soberly, dressed.

His mouth was thin and apt to droop at the corners, and his nose was an odd lumpy shape. But he was kind, Amanda persuaded herself. She was now nineteen years old and often looked younger. Had Lord Hawksborough, or his mother, or society for that matter, guessed there was any possibility of an attachment between Lord Box and Miss Colby, then Lord Hawksborough would have forbidden the friendship, as would his mother; society would have tittered cruelly, and the press would have lampooned Miss Colby with malicious wit.

But as it was, everyone supposed the elderly lord to be courting Aunt Matilda.

Unfortunately, Aunt Matilda thought so too.

Since love and romance among the elderly—and anyone in his fifties in an era when few people reached their three score years and ten *was* elderly—was totally beyond Amanda's comprehension, she failed to notice the heaving of Aunt Matilda's scrawny bosom every time Lord Box came to call.

As to Lord Box being in love with *herself*, Amanda would have found that idea just as ridiculous. She hoped Lord Box looked on her as a young companion who would brighten his declining years.

Lord Hawksborough sometimes wondered why Amanda wasted so much time with her aunt's inamorato instead of looking at any of the attractive young men who danced with her at parties and balls, but not for one moment did he think she planned marriage.

Since that unfortunate night when he had returned from abroad, followed by the unfortunate morning when he had so far forgotten himself as to nearly rape Miss Colby, Lord Hawksborough had persuaded himself that he had forgotten her entirely. Lady Mary seemed to stay more at his house than she did at her own, and so he wearily decided they may as well get married in June. Lady Mary gained a warm kiss from him when she said shyly that since she had no close female relatives, she would like Susan and Miss Colby to be maids of honour.

Susan accepted the news with pleasure, Miss Colby with affected pleasure.

Miss Colby then shut herself up in her room and cried for that which was gone, never to return, and then set about charming Lord Box as hard as she could.

When Amanda felt Lord Box was on the point of proposing, she asked Aunt Matilda how that lady would feel about sharing a household with Lord Box.

Aunt Matilda was trying on new caps when Amanda asked her the question. Her eyes lit up and she exclaimed, "Darling child! Ever so perceptive. Why, you must know it is what my heart is set on."

"I wanted to talk to you," said Amanda seriously, "because I hoped you would understand it is something I would like above all things."

Aunt Matilda kissed Amanda fondly, her eyes misting with tears. "You are a good and generous girl, Amanda," she said. "It is also wonderful to know our future is secure. Does . . . does Richard know? Richard is sometimes not quite . . ."

"Richard is in Oxford," said Amanda. "He need not know anything until he reads the announcement. I do not think he would understand."

"Just what I thought." Aunt Matilda nodded her head wisely. "Those young men *will* try to play head of the household."

And so both ladies, firmly convinced that the other was pleased over her forthcoming marriage to Lord Box, parted with warm protestations of love and friendship.

For his part, Lord Box was only too eager to propose to Amanda before the Season began. He was well aware that everyone thought he was courting Aunt Matilda, and encouraged that idea because he did not want all the old stories about how he had buried three young wives getting to Amanda's ears. He had told her about only one.

He was sure Lord Hawksborough would give his permission. He was no relative to the girl, and, by rights, Lord Box should have asked the girl's aunt. But he was frightened that the old lady would think herself jilted and would therefore refuse her consent.

But his supposed pursuit of the aunt made it remarkably hard to see Miss Colby alone. At last he thought he saw his chance.

Napoleon had escaped from Elba, and no one was in the least surprised, except the British government. Lord Hawksborough was busy enjoying the doubtful pleasure of saying "I told you so" at various high-ranking meetings.

A ball was to be held that evening at Lady Crompton's mansion in Kensington. Lord Hawksborough had said it was doubtful whether he would be able to attend. At the last moment, Aunt Matilda found a cold in the head too severe to allow her to go, and so Lord Box had the pleasure of escorting Amanda, Susan, and Lady Mary.

Amanda felt unbearably tense, for she knew this was the evening he would propose and she intended to give him every opportunity to do so.

Susan was morose because she was no longer in fashion, having unwittingly crossed swords with Mr. Brummell, who had taken her in dislike, and whoever Mr. Brummell took in dislike was doomed. Now she was wishing she had not been so cold to Mr. Dalzell and was grumpily inclined to blame the whole thing on Amanda's bad advice.

Lady Mary was as pleasant as ever, but her dislike of Amanda was always there, below the surface, creating an uneasy atmosphere.

Amanda's elderly beau did not like to dance and so she kindly agreed to sit out two dances with him, hoping he would take the opportunity to propose and get it over with.

Her nasty inner voice pointed out that the last time she had felt thus was before a visit to the dentist.

It was a warm, blustery night. The ballroom was alive with rumours about the fate of the French King. One said he had been taken at Lille, another that he had gone to Tournay. But one thing was plain. Napoleon Bonaparte had been declared a rebel and a traitor by the French government and a price of 100,000 louis d'or set upon his head.

Amanda indulged in a brief fantasy of capturing Napoleon single-handed, collecting the reward from a grateful French government, and settling down to a life of blissful spinsterhood at Fox End.

Perhaps Lord Box would not live very long, she thought, and then was appalled at her own evil mercenary wishes.

So that when his lordship led her gently from the ballroom and through the hall and into an anteroom, Amanda smiled on him in quite an enchanting way to make up for having wished him dead only a few moments before.

At first, all went very smoothly. To the faint strains of a waltz drifting from the ballroom on the hot scented air, Lord Box creaked down on one knee and formally asked Miss Colby for her hand in marriage.

Miss Colby formally accepted.

Lord Box rose to his feet.

Amanda brushed down her skirts in the way she used to do at Fox End when she had just completed a difficult and distasteful household task, and murmured that they should be returning to join the other guests.

Lord Box seized her in his arms.

Before she could protest, he had crushed his mouth down on hers. Fighting for breath and assailed with nausea, Amanda finally broke free.

"My lord," she gasped, "you are too warm in your attentions."

"Frightened you, did I?" he said heartily. "You'll get used to it, m'dear. For I mean to get a lot warmer than that. Not bad for such an old boy, heh?"

He squeezed her around the waist and peered lasciviously down her *décolletage*.

"My lord," protested Amanda. "We must go. I am not chaperoned."

"Don't worry. I'll talk to Hawksborough as soon as possible. Never could stand long engagements. Get married about the same time as Hawksborough, heh? Make it a double wedding."

Amanda closed her eyes tightly, seeing a vision of a radiant Lady Mary and a handsome Lord Hawksborough standing before the altar, while she stood next to them, flanked by this elderly satyr.

She edged away from him, a voice crying in her head, "What have I done?"

Fortunately, Lord Box decided to go back to the

ballroom and Amanda could only be glad when a young man came up to claim her hand for the next dance.

As she performed the steps of the quadrille, she saw out of the corner of one green eye that Lord Hawksborough had just entered the ballroom.

And worse.

Lord Box immediately went forward and took him by the arm and started to talk to him intently.

As soon as the dance was over, Amanda looked wildly round for a means of escape.

It was then that Mr. Bertram Dalzell came up and demanded the pleasure of a few words with her in private.

By now so upset that she was deaf and blind to the conventions, Amanda led him back to the anteroom where Lord Box had so recently made his proposal.

Amanda sat down and Mr. Dalzell proceeded to pace up and down the room.

At last he came to a stop and faced her. "I am desolate, Miss Colby."

"I am so very sorry, Mr.—"

"Susan told me you had advised her not to see or talk to me again."

Amanda blushed. "I thought it was good advice, since she did not love you, Mr. Dalzell."

"I thought my heart was broken," he said, sinking down on a chair and running his hands through his guinea-gold hair.

Despite her distress and embarrassment, Amanda could not help noticing that Mr. Dalzell's hair sprang back naturally into a fashionable hairstyle despite his tousling of it. He was very beautiful and had probably been *born* looking fashionable, she thought.

She set herself to try to extricate herself from this latest predicament as soon as possible.

"Mr. Dalzell," she said firmly, "if Susan's affections had been truly engaged, then nothing I could possibly have said would have changed her mind."

"Oh, so wise," he murmured, staring at her.

"Thank you," said Amanda uneasily, wondering if some of these totty-headed people who graced London society were a result of inbreeding. "Then," she said firmly, "all I can do is apologise for any damage I may have done."

"The only damage you have done," he said intensely, "is to my heart."

"Oh," said Amanda wretchedly, thinking of her own pain. Was Lord Hawksborough looking for her even now to give her his blessing to her forthcoming marriage? She stood up. Mr. Dalzell stood up at the same time.

"If it is any consolation," said Amanda in a low voice, "I share your feelings. I know exactly the pain—"

"You do? Miss Colby! I had not dared to hope. I saw you from afar, *worshipped* you from afar. Your slight figure, your bewitching eyes, your charming smile."

"Mr. Dalzell!" shrieked Amanda.

"Not 'Mr. Dalzell,' " he breathed. " 'Bertram'!"

And with that, he seized her in his arms and covered her face with kisses.

"Amanda!"

Mr. Dalzell dropped his arms and Amanda backed away hurriedly.

Lord Hawksborough and Susan stood in the doorway.

"So *that* was why you were so free with your advice," raged Susan. "You wanted him for yourself!"

"Quiet, Susan," said Lord Hawksborough. "Miss Colby,

while you are a guest under my roof, you will please observe the conventions, since it seems that some gentlemen cannot.

"Mr. Dalzell, you will kindly escort my sister back to the ballroom. I wish to have a few words in private with Miss Colby."

Amanda gave a hollow groan and sat down again.

Mr. Dalzell took a step toward her but Amanda snapped crossly, "Oh, go *away*. I don't care for you a bit. It's someone else I love, which is why I said I shared your feelings. Just go *away*!"

"You deliberately misled me—" began Mr. Dalzell.

"Miss Colby said 'go away,' " remarked Lord Hawksborough. "Do it."

"Come, Susan," said Mr. Dalzell with great hauteur.

" 'Miss Fitzgerald' to you," snapped the sorely tried viscount, but Susan was flashing a triumphant look at Amanda and leading Mr. Dalzell from the room.

Lord Hawksborough pulled up a chair and sat facing Amanda so that their knees were nearly touching.

"Now," he said very softly. "Would you care to enlighten me?"

"About what?" asked Amanda, hoping if she stalled for time that there would be some interruption. She nervously opened and shut her fan, until he reached forward and took it from her.

"Look at me," he said.

"No." Amanda mulishly studied her hands.

He put a long finger under her chin and forced her head up.

"I am appalled, yes, *appalled*, to find that an elderly rip who has buried three wives, and whom I tolerated in my household because I thought he was paying court to your aunt, should hail me tonight and ask my permission to pay his addresses to you.

"I thought he was foxed and told him to go and take a damper. He told me gleefully that he had already proposed and been accepted. His ugly old mouth was stained with rouge, and I notice you are no longer wearing any. I told him I refused my permission. He pointed out he had only asked as a courtesy and didn't really need it, so I put it another way.

"I said I would kill him if I saw him near my home again."

Amanda jerked her head away. "What if I love him?"

"Then you belong in Bedlam. You are trying to hide your eyes now, but when I said I had forbidden my permission, I read relief there. I know what it is," he added in a more kindly tone. "You believed, like everyone else, that he was courting your aunt."

"No," said Amanda in a small voice. "I didn't. And I would have married him because I thought he merely wanted a young companion, and so I accepted his proposal. Then he kissed me."

"And?"

"And it revolted me," said Amanda in a low voice.

"But why did you encourage him in the first place? There are many young men about."

"Money."

"Are you so greedy that you would contemplate sharing a marriage bed with that old goat?"

"I *told* you," said Amanda, her eyes glistening with tears. "And I thought he was too old to . . . to be interested in . . . in that side of things."

"One is never too old. Your aunt must not learn of this. Do you not know she is in love with him?"

"Yes. No. I mean, not passionate love, surely."

"Oh, yes, surely. I shall make certain Lord Box takes himself off to rusticate in the country. Your aunt will be sad, but she will not be so heartbroken as she would be if she knew how she had been used. Yes, *used*, Amanda."

"I'm sorry," mumbled Amanda, hanging her head. "So if you have finished . . ."

"No, I have not finished. What the deuce were you doing in young Dalzell's arms?"

Amanda wearily told him of the mistake she had made.

"You tell my sister not to marry without love, and yet you seem prepared to do so yourself."

"As *you* are."

"We are not discussing me," he said angrily.

"Your sister can afford to marry for love," said Amanda. "I cannot. We cannot stay as your mother's pensioners forever. Furthermore, when you are married, Lady Mary will be living permanently in Berkeley Square. I think you will find she does not wish us underfoot."

"You must not panic," he said gently. "The Season will soon begin. You must rate your charms a little higher. I do not think you have really *looked* at one young man since you came to London."

"I don't *want* to get married," said Amanda passionately. "I want to be a spinster with a fixed income and live at Fox End till I die."

"If that is your desire, I will give you an allowance."

"Thank you. I am prepared to accept your charity, your mother's charity, for a short time. But I could not live the rest of my life that way. I have already behaved in a disgracefully irresponsible manner in trying to gain money in a dishonest way," said Amanda, thinking miserably of the robbery.

"You are too hard on yourself," he said, thinking she was still talking about Lord Box. He was experiencing a heady feeling of elation. She did not love that old fool, Box. She did not love Dalzell either.

"You seem to know much about love," he mocked, "since you have been advising my sister. If you are not in love with Box, then whom are you in love with, Amanda?"

She hung her head. "You're in love with him," sneered her inner voice, and she said aloud, "Oh, no!"

"Whom are you in love with," he pursued, his voice caressing, and leaning forward so that his mouth was very near her own.

Amanda tore her eyes away from his mouth. She racked her brain for the names of the young men she had danced with.

What was the name of the fellow who had partnered her in the quadrille? Fairish hair, grey eyes, stocky figure. Carruthers! That was it. Mr. Peter Carruthers.

"Mr. Carruthers," said Amanda with that sharp, wary twist of her head he knew so well.

"Liar," he said softly. He placed his hands on her knees and leaned forward and put his mouth gently against her own. Amanda sat very still, willing herself to feel nothing.

At last he drew back, a puzzled, intent look on his face. "Let us go." He rose abruptly, and Amanda jumped to her feet and stumbled, knocking the light gilt chair he had been sitting on flying.

She caught hold of his shoulder to steady herself and he put an arm about her waist and looked down at her.

She was wearing the sea-green gown in which he had first seen her. Her eyes were wide and green and gold.

He quite suddenly kissed her again, this time fiercely and insistently until he felt her response, felt her answering surge of passion, felt her lips begin to part beneath his own. He gave a little groan in the back of his throat and held her more tightly.

There came the high, petulant sound of a female voice outside, saying, "Perhaps he is in here. I've looked everywhere else."

He drew back quickly, but not quite quickly enough.

Lady Mary opened the door in time to catch the *sense* of withdrawal between the guilty pair.

"I have been looking everywhere for you," she said, her eyes fixed and glaring. "Have you forgotten our dance?"

"My apologies, Mary. Miss Colby received an unfortunate proposal of marriage and I had to turn her suitor down."

"Why, pray? You are not her kin."

He went forward and took her arm and tucked it in his and smiled down at her. "I know, Mary, but under the circumstances, I see myself in the light of guardian to the young Colbys."

Lady Mary gave a laugh, slightly reassured, but her eyes still went to where Amanda stood.

"Are you coming, Miss Colby?" said the viscount over his shoulder.

"Later," said Amanda.

For a long time Amanda stood and lectured herself. Lord Hawksborough was *not* behaving like a gentleman. Was she to let him kiss and caress her anytime he pleased? If he cared one rap for her, he would endeavour to cancel his engagement. She knew it was almost impossible for a gentleman to cry off once the date was set and the invitations sent out. But if he loved her, he could surely manage somehow.

But common sense told her he did not love her; he was attracted to her, but not enough to wish to wed her. Then, the Colbys were not aristocracy, only gentry, so he would not ally his name with that of such an undistinguished family.

Lord Hawksborough's elevation to the peerage had been of recent date, but the Fitzgeralds belonged to the untitled aristocracy and were considered too grand to have ever even bothered scrambling for a title.

At last Amanda raised her chin and marched into the ballroom. She would flirt with Mr. Carruthers and see if *that* might give his philandering lordship something to think about.

Lord Hawksborough was tired. He had had a long day at the Foreign Office, and was about to gather the party together and suggest they go home, when his hostess, Lady Crompton, fluttered up to him, her prominent eyes bulging ever more with excitement.

"Well," she exclaimed, "so Boney escaped just as you said he would!"

"I do not recall saying such a thing," said Lord Hawksborough.

"But of course you did. Lady Mary told all of us. 'Charles saw Napoleon on Elba, actually talked to the monster,' that's what she said, and she said you had told the government he would escape but they would not listen to you."

Suddenly and vividly Lord Hawksborough remembered telling Amanda about his visit to Elba and how Lady

Mary had surprised them but had sworn she had not heard a word.

"I think you must be mistaken," he said stiffly. "I told Lady Mary no such thing."

His hostess's attention was caught by another guest. Lord Hawksborough immediately went in search of his fiancée and taxed her bitterly with spreading dangerous gossip and with listening at doors.

He was savagely glad to have something to blame her for. Normally he was the one who was always being made to feel guilty.

"But you told that Colby creature," said Lady Mary, opening her eyes to their widest. "I assumed you would tell me too, and when you did not, I gathered you had merely forgotten. Why, after all, would you confide such intelligence to a virtual stranger if it were a secret?"

Without being rude, Lord Hawksborough felt he could not truthfully reply to her question—the truth being he instinctively knew Amanda would not gossip, just as he had instinctively known Lady Mary would.

"Let us go home," he replied instead. "I'll be glad when this evening is over. Miss Colby can be very taxing."

Lady Mary smiled warmly at him. "You will soon have children of your own to worry about, Charles," she murmured. "You are too softhearted. You must let me handle things. As soon as we are married, I will send the taxing and tiresome Miss Colby packing."

Lord Hawksborough opened his mouth to reply, but she had moved off in front of him and was already making their adieux.

It was a grim journey home. Susan was furious with

Amanda for "stealing my beau," as she hissed in an undertone; Lady Mary now decided that Amanda Colby was a dangerous girl and hated her accordingly; and Lord Hawksborough was emanating worry and tension. He was worried because he had told Lady Mary about Lord Box's proposal to Amanda. He hoped Lady Mary would not tell Aunt Matilda. He would warn her as soon as he got her alone.

Aunt Matilda and Mrs. Fitzgerald, who had stayed to keep her company, were waiting up in the Red Drawing Room. Aunt Matilda very much rouged and wearing a new cap. Her face fell when the party entered.

"Why did you not bring my dear Lord Box back with you?" she cried, while Mrs. Fitzgerald smiled indulgently.

"Your dear Lord Box proposed marriage to Miss Colby and was refused." Lady Mary laughed. "Quite right, too. Wicked old rip. Pretending to be courting you, Miss Pettifor, when he was after younger game."

Aunt Matilda's mouth fell open.

"Oh, no," whispered Amanda.

Aunt Matilda suddenly jumped to her feet, two red spots of colour burning on her cheeks. "You!" she said to Amanda. "You tried to *steal* him. He loved me. Me!"

"Oh, Miss Colby prefers other ladies' gentlemen," teased Lady Mary, enjoying herself immensely.

"Yes, she does that," sneered Susan. "She advised me to drop Dalzell and then she stole him herself."

Poor Amanda started to protest incoherently, "I didn't. I wouldn't. I couldn't. I can't bear it."

Mrs. Fitzgerald arose with a sort of massive dignity. "Come with me, Miss Colby," she said.

"I think I can explain," protested Lord Hawksborough.

"No," said Mrs. Fitzgerald with awful hauteur. "On this occasion I will deal with matters myself."

Amanda followed her from the room, praying for an earthquake to shake the house to pieces, for a tidal wave to come roaring up the Thames, for anything to help her to escape from the confrontation about to begin.

"Sit down," barked Mrs. Fitzgerald.

"Thank you. I prefer to stand," said Amanda.

"Very well. Now, listen to me. You are in this house simply because you are Matilda's niece. Her welfare comes first. To go and break her heart by taking away her beau is the outside of enough."

"I did not know Aunt Matilda's affections were seriously engaged," replied Amanda, trying to keep her voice from trembling. "I would never dream of trying to annex the affections of any gentleman who—"

"Fustian. I know what has been happening. You have been casting languishing looks at my son. Aye, well you may blush! That sweet child Lady Mary told me it was sad to see the way you dote upon him. He has no interest in you. Charles has always flirted, but until he met Lady Mary, he never had any serious intentions towards any female. There is no danger of your taking his affections away from dear Lady Mary. What I am complaining about is that you are *trying* to do so. My servants tell me you have been closeted with him alone on several occasions, once even in his bedchamber. His bedchamber!" repeated Mrs. Fitzgerald, her eyes flashing. "Now, I do not know what free-and-easy manners you may have adopted in the country, but here you are expected to behave like a young lady. . . . Are you still a virgin?"

"Of course!" squeaked Amanda, putting her hands up to her flushed face.

"For the sake of your aunt, I am prepared to overlook your behaviour. But should I find you flirting with my son, with any of Susan's beaux, or with anyone your aunt shows a *tendre* for—since age seems to be no barrier in your case, miss—I will send you packing."

"Why do you assume the fault is all on my side?" cried Amanda. "Lord Hawksborough has . . ." She bit her lip. To tell this stern matron that her son had passionately held her in his arms would only make matters worse.

"Do not try to place the blame elsewhere." Mrs. Fitzgerald thrust her jaw forward. "It does not become you. From now on, wherever you go, you will be strictly chaperoned. And you will no longer ride with Susan in the Park. I do not think you fitting company for my daughter."

"Mrs. Fitzgerald," said Amanda desperately, "you must understand, I am not the monster you would have me."

"Your future behaviour is the only thing that will make me change my mind," snapped Mrs. Fitzgerald. "I think the company will excuse you. Please go to your room."

And Amanda meekly went. It was horrible, it was unfair. She had only meant to do things for the best. It had been for Richard's and Aunt Matilda's sakes as much as her own that she had encouraged Lord Box in his attentions. She felt a superstitious shudder run through her. Perhaps this was divine retribution for the highway robbery. Perhaps these mistakes and humiliations would go on and on until she confessed.

She sat beside the fire in her bedroom, listening to the

dreary call of the watch, marking the half-hours, wishing she had the courage to run away.

If only she and Richard had been born into a lower social station, then they would have been trained to work. Richard would find work eventually, but his studies at the university had only just begun, and it would be a shame if he had to forgo them.

The door opened and she looked up in surprise as Mrs. Fitzgerald entered the room. Amanda cringed in her chair, and then got to her feet and stood as stiff as a ramrod in front of the fire. Had Mrs. Fitzgerald come to give her another lecture? Enough was enough.

But Mrs. Fitzgerald said mildly, "Sit down, Amanda. I am not going to lecture you anymore."

Amanda looked at her anxiously and then did as she was bid. Mrs. Fitzgerald sat down opposite and sighed.

"I do not know quite how to begin," she said awkwardly, looking as shy as a massive domineering woman can ever look. "I have been talking to my son, or rather, he has been talking to me. He has confessed that he has behaved towards you in a manner unbefitting a gentleman—in short, he has been flirting with you. He says you did not encourage him in the slightest, in fact, that you did not need to."

Amanda felt quite weak at the knees.

"He, by rights, should terminate his engagement to Lady Mary. But he cannot. It is a point of honour, you see. Furthermore, he believes Lady Mary to be deeply in love with him, although she has done several things since your arrival that seem to have disillusioned him about her completely."

"Lady Mary has never been married before?" asked Amanda, thinking of that lady's twenty-eight summers.

"No. It is a sad story. She was engaged twice. The first gentleman was killed in a duel; the second ran away to the Continent a day before the wedding. Charles did not learn of this until a week ago. So you see, she will not release him. She has little money of her own, and my son has a considerable fortune."

"Then she cannot love him!" exclaimed Amanda.

"I think she does." Mrs. Fitzgerald smiled. The smile transformed her whole face. "But you should not be too hard on her. Charles tells me you were prepared to marry Lord Box in order to secure a future for Richard and your aunt. He explained to me that you were unaware your aunt's affections were seriously engaged, thinking us older people too withered to indulge in the headstrong passions of youth."

"How is my aunt?" asked Amanda in a low voice.

"She is still in great distress. Charles says cynically he thinks she is beginning to enjoy the drama and that may be the case. What I am come for, Miss Colby, is to proffer my apologies. But, I beg of you, avoid my son. It will not make his lot easier to bear. As a man of honour and a gentleman, he is honour-bound to marry Lady Mary."

"And if he were not?" asked Amanda in a voice barely above a whisper. "Would he marry me?"

"That I do not know, and it is useless to speculate thereon. Perhaps your attraction for him lies simply in the fact you are forbidden fruit. Gentlemen always lust after what they should not have."

Amanda hung her head and Mrs. Fitzgerald looked at her with a certain sympathy.

"Has Charles shown any actual love for you?"

Passion, Amanda thought, a certain teasing mockery, a certain warmth. But love?"

Slowly she shook her head.

"Then it should make your task easier," said Mrs. Fitzgerald. "Goodness knows, I have my hands full with Susan. I do not think telling her lies about how attractive she looks has done the slightest good at all."

"It is better than constantly telling her she is plain," flashed Amanda. "Forgive me, ma'am," she added in a contrite voice, "but I fear Susan's clumsiness and gaucheries came about because she was accustomed to thinking herself plain."

"I will decide how to bring up my daughter, *if* you please, and I am not in need of advice from a chit like you," said Mrs. Fitzgerald tartly, reverting to her former manner. "I was a great beauty in my youth. Susan takes after her father."

Lady Mary removed her ear from the other side of the door and slid off quietly along the passageway. She was consumed with rage and jealousy. She did not give a rap if Lord Hawksborough married her reluctantly, just so long as he *did* marry her.

Lady Mary had put considerable work into securing him. She had adopted a free-and-easy and open manner which she instinctively knew would sit well with him. She could not risk being jilted again. She was extravagant and coveted Lord Hawksborough's money to buy beautiful gowns and jewels. Her first fiancé had been killed in a duel after he was accused of cheating at cards. Her second had complained she was out to send him into the River Tick since she had already started to make inroads in his fortune before the wedding.

And then he had run away. Her face still burned as

she remembered the shame of that day. The engagement to Hawksborough had proved to the Polite World that she was an attractive woman. She had seized the prize from under the pretty noses of so many. She did not love Lord Hawksborough. But she was determined to keep a close guard on him until the day of the wedding.

Amanda Colby must be removed. There must be some way to discredit her. Lady Mary sat down to plot and scheme.

8

The Season seemed to be hurtling towards Amanda at a tremendous rate. Mrs. Fitzgerald had secured vouchers for both Susan and Amanda to Almack's—those famous assembly rooms which were the high temple of London fashion.

Relieved that the repercussions over her marriage proposal were not nearly so great as she had feared, Amanda began conscientiously to look for a beau. Having said she loved young Mr. Carruthers, she decided he would do as well as anyone. He was a cheerful, unaffected young man of twenty-three. He was not possessed of any great degree of intelligence, but he made up for it by being unflaggingly good-natured. He seemed happy to accept the role of Amanda's beau, although he had no serious intentions of marriage. He supposed he would become married sometime in the vague future, but for the moment he was content to squire the vivacious and undemanding Miss Colby anywhere she wished.

Lady Mary had been unexpectedly friendly. Amanda did not trust her, but was prepared to accept her surface

character, since she still felt guiltily that there had been
some truth in Mrs. Fitzgerald's original lecture: she *had*
been casting languishing eyes at Lord Hawksborough.

Richard came down from Oxford for a weekend and
paid court to Susan, which quite restored that young
lady's *amour propre*, and she graciously agreed to resume
her rides with Amanda in the Park.

Aunt Matilda had not quite forgiven Amanda and
had returned for a while to her old habit of sleeping too
much. She was convinced her lover had been stolen
from her. The whirl of London fashion had rather gone
to her head, and in a mildly crazy way, she regarded
her niece as a rival.

But a few bullying and bracing words from Mrs.
Fitzgerald at least got Aunt Matilda back on her feet
and out into the world again.

Amanda was out riding early one morning with
Susan and Mr. Carruthers. They were hailed by Colonel
John Withers, the Hussar officer who had been of the
party the evening they had gone to see Kean in *Othello*.
He engaged Susan in conversation, leaving Mr. Carruthers
to ride side by side with Amanda a little way ahead.

Amanda was wearing a smart blue velvet riding habit
which she felt became her. It gave her confidence to
sound out Mr. Carruthers on the subject of marriage.
She felt it was time the young man showed signs of
popping the question. So far he had been about as
loverlike towards her as her brother, Richard.

"I confess I am dreading the Season," said Amanda,
watching the spring sun burn through the mist which
snaked around the boles of the old trees in Hyde Park.
Daffodils grew in the tussocky grass, and the young
leaves were fairy green. Shafts of sunlight, diffused and

broadened by the mist, turned the Park into a panto-
mime transformation scene.

Any moment, the gauze would rise, the trees would
melt away, and there they would be in Prince Charming's
palace, and Prince Charming would be wearing her—it
was always a woman—glittering uniform of tinsel and
silver epaulettes, the sort of thing poor Prinny used to
wear before his mentor, Mr. Brummell, persuaded him
it was vulgar.

"Nothing to fear about the Season," said Peter
Carruthers.

"It is different for a man," replied Amanda, slowing
her horse to an ambling pace.

"How so?"

"Gentlemen do not *need* to get married," pointed out
Amanda.

He frowned deeply, as if faced by a mathematical
problem of great complexity. Then his face cleared.
"Ladies don't have to either," he said triumphantly.
"Do you care to gallop, Miss Colby?"

"No," said Amanda crossly. "And it is *not* the same
for ladies. What else can a lady do, if she does not
marry? She can become a governess, someone neither
fish nor fowl, despised by the mistress and the upper
servants. She can become a companion, and measure
out her days holding some cross old lady's knitting."

Mr. Carruthers reined in his horse to give the matter
full attention. A shaft of sunlight gilded his curly fair
hair and sent prisms of light sparkling from the large
diamond in his stock.

At last he turned an awestruck face to Amanda. "By
George, Miss Colby," he said in admiration. "I always

thought you was a deep 'un. Now, *I* would never have thought of a thing like that."

Short of saying to this cackle-brained lump of amiability, "Will you marry me?" I don't really see what else I can say, thought Amanda.

Nonetheless, she tried again. "I must marry, you see. I only hope I can find someone kind and good-natured."

"Like me," said Mr. Carruthers jovially, and Amanda sighed with relief. "Tell you what, I'll look around m'friends. Now, I don't plan to get leg-shackled for a few years, but I've noticed that some of 'em are suddenly struck with the thought. Take Philip Otley. One minute, biggest rake in town. Gets moody one night. Looks down at the dregs of his fifth bottle and says, 'I'm going to get married.' Just like that! 'Who?' I asks. 'Don't know,' says he, 'but anyone will do.' So there you are. Would you care to gallop, Miss Colby?"

"Oh, *yes*," sighed Amanda. She let him fly off ahead and stayed where she was, wrapped in thought. She had wasted *weeks* on Mr. Carruthers. And she had all but proposed to him. Good heavens! What if he went about the clubs saying Amanda Colby was desperate for a husband!

She spurred her horse and galloped after him, only to find when she finally caught up that she need not have troubled. Mr. Carruthers had already forgotten the whole conversation.

Amanda began to feel downcast. Catching a husband was going to be very difficult. Oh, if there was only a way of making money that did not involve marriage!

Without really taking into consideration to whom she was speaking, she voiced this thought aloud to Lady

Mary, simply because Lady Mary happened to be the only female around when she arrived home.

"There is a very easy way," said Lady Mary casually. "But I suppose you know about it."

Amanda shook her head.

"Well, it depends on your luck at the card table. . . ."

"I am *very* lucky."

"Then there are gaming houses for ladies, all most genteel, I assure you."

"But how does one gain an introduction to one of those houses?"

"In the case of the best ones, by invitation. You see, a certain noble lady will send out cards of invitation, just as if to an ordinary card party. That way she can escape the attention of the law. Not that there is anything precisely *illegal*, you understand.

"All the best people go. I have an invitation to Lady Mannering's tonight, but I have refused it because we are bound for the opera. Of course, I could go anytime during the night because the play will not finish until dawn but—ah, me—I do not have your luck."

Lady Mary rummaged around in her diamond-shaped reticule and brought out a plain card with black embossed lettering. "There, you see . . . I think I hear dear Charles in the hall. Excuse me, Miss Colby."

Amanda slowly turned the invitation card over in her hands. It was oddly worded in that no one in particular was invited. "Admit bearer" was inscribed in small, curly script at the bottom.

Amanda wondered and wondered whether to go and try her luck. She decided to leave her fate up to the gods. If Lady Mary asked for her invitation back, then she would not go. But as the day wore on, calls were made in the company of Aunt Matilda, Mrs. Fitzgerald, and Lady Mary, but Lady Mary did not mention the gambling house again.

They were about to set out for the opera in the evening. Lord Hawksborough had said he would meet them there. He avoided Amanda and always seemed only to see her when they were both surrounded by a crowd of people. Aunt Matilda was scanning a letter which had come from Mr. Cartwright-Browne by the morning post. She had put off reading it, because, she said, it would no doubt be full of the boring details of yet another lawsuit against Mr. Brotherington.

But as her eyes moved over the crabbed handwriting, her long sheeplike face fell and the end of her nose began to turn pink, a sure sign of distress.

"What is it, Aunt?" asked Amanda.

"It is Mr. Cartwright-Browne. He wishes to terminate the lease of Fox End. I doubt if we shall find another tenant to take it for a mere three months. I suppose I must give in gracefully, or no doubt he will try to sue *me*. We could have done with the extra . . ."

Aunt Matilda bit her lip and glanced away from Mrs. Fitzgerald, but everyone knew what she had been about to say.

They most certainly could have done with the extra money.

"I have the headache," said Amanda suddenly. "I feel I cannot attend the opera tonight. Present my excuses to Lord Hawksborough."

"You are certainly very flushed," said Mrs. Fitzgerald.

"Oh, I think she should most certainly lie down," said Lady Mary sweetly, and Amanda looked at her with sudden suspicion.

Did Lady Mary guess what she, Amanda, planned to do?

But that was impossible.

In the privacy of her bedroom, she studied the invitation again. Montague Street. Not so very far away. She could take a hack.

Amanda sat and thought furiously. She felt she did not have the courage to visit a strange house on her own. There was no one she could ask to go with her.

Susan!

Susan was staying at home because she said she detested opera. All that caterwauling and screeching gave her the vapours.

After a search, Amanda found Susan in the Green Drawing Room, lying on a sofa in front of the fire, reading a letter and eating chocolates.

"You didn't go either," said Susan, thrusting the letter under a cushion. "What's the matter? No other men to steal?"

"Oh, Susan, do not be at odds with me," said Amanda. "I need your help."

"Fire away," said Susan, sitting up and looking more amiable. "Richard told me to take care of you, anyway."

"Richard? When did you see him?"

"I didn't," said Susan, blushing. "He . . . er . . . wrote."

"How is he? What does he say?"

"Oh, this and that and t'other," said Susan airily. "Tell me your problem."

So Amanda outlined the Colby predicament. She said she was desperately in need of money, and winning money at cards would mean she did not have to get married.

Susan began to look bored. She detested card games almost as much as she detested the opera.

"And don't you see," Amanda went on desperately, "Mr. Cartwright-Browne has left or is leaving Fox End, so if we had money, Richard and I could return, and you could come with us. We could go fishing and shooting and you would not need to go to balls or parties."

"So what do you want me to do?" asked Susan with sudden enthusiasm.

Amanda held out the invitation. "Come to this gaming house with me."

Susan scowled at it. "Lady Mannering . . . she is not quite *bon ton* but I have not heard anything really bad about her. Very well. We will take the vis-à-vis as if we are going on a call. If we go and get a hack, the servants might gossip."

Amanda went to give her a friendly hug, but Susan said gruffly, "Keep your distance. I still do not trust you."

"Oh, *Susan!*" said Amanda, much exasperated. "You never wanted Mr. Dalzell anyway. You're like a dog with a bone it doesn't really want."

"But such a pretty bone," remarked Susan. "Come along. It's all very exciting. But I shall watch, mind you. Do not expect me to play. You have money?"

"Yes, I've saved most of my allowance."

Despite Amanda's secret fears of finding herself in a smoke-laden den of iniquity full of painted women, they set out.

The gambling club turned out to be almost disappointingly refined.

Amanda handed over the card and introduced herself

to Lady Mannering, a grim-faced woman of uncertain years who looked like a governess. They left their cloaks and rather shyly entered the gaming room.

To Amanda's relief, she recognised several of the ladies present. She sat down at a faro table and Susan stood behind her, occasionally sighing and shuffling her feet.

Amanda played and played. Susan eventually moved over to a sofa in the corner and fell asleep.

Sometimes Amanda won a little, sometimes she lost a little, and then, quite amazingly, she began to win and win. When she found she had won the incredible sum of five hundred guineas, she tore herself away from the table and awoke Susan. Lady Mannering relaxed her grim visage to congratulate Miss Colby on her luck. Miss Colby should return the next night, she said. The stakes would be higher, a deal of very rich ladies were expected to attend, and there would be a champagne supper. Amanda looked excited. Susan yawned cavernously in Lady Mannering's face and said grumpily that once was enough.

"But I have won five hundred guineas," exclaimed Amanda as they jogged home.

"Then keep it," said Susan. "You'll lose it if you go back tomorrow."

"No. Just one more time. And *please come* with me. I'll . . . I'll pay you."

"Just invite me to that place of yours in Hardforshire," said Susan with a reluctant smile. "And take five of those guineas and give them to John coachman to keep his mouth shut. If he gossips in the kitchens, cook will tell the housekeeper and she will tell the lady's maid, Mathers, and Mathers will tell Mama."

The coachman not only promised to keep quiet but also let them in by a back door to the house around by the mews and so they were able to creep quietly up the stairs unnoticed.

"I think the headache must be becoming infectious," said Lord Hawksborough to his fiancée, Lady Mary Dane, as they sat out in the refreshment room at Lord Tavistock's ball the following night. "Both Susan and Miss Colby seem struck with it at the same time."

"Then it is a mercy," said Lady Mary tartly. "I feel like a governess, having to be constantly in the company of these pimply schoolgirls."

"I would call neither Susan nor Miss Colby pimply."

"Their *souls* are pimply and covered with chalk and ink blots," said Lady Mary, raising her hand to the sapphire pendant that hung between her breasts and hoping that his lordship's eyes would be guided by the gesture and so divert his mind to a more interesting subject.

Lady Mary had reluctantly agreed to give the next dance to Lord Tavistock but was hoping he would not remember the fact, since she was not in the ballroom, but to her irritation, she found him at her elbow reminding her of the promise.

Lord Hawksborough watched her go. He found himself disliking her more and more and wondered irritably if he would have been quite comfortable in his engagement had Amanda not entered his life.

He saw Mrs. Burke, a notorious old gossip, bearing down on him and made a move to escape. But he was too slow and she was upon him, her old eyes snapping with malice and mischief.

"Well, Hawksborough," she said. "You ought to keep an eye on that sister of yours. And little Miss Colby. Too young to be fleeced in a gambling hell."

Lord Hawksborough took out his quizzing glass and stared awfully at Mrs. Burke. "What are you talking about?" he said acidly.

"Sally Struthers-Benson was at Lady Mannering's hell in Montague Street last night and she said Miss Colby was gambling like Sheridan, while your sister egged her on. They allowed Miss Colby to win. They always do that the first time, you know. Got her coming back tonight to fleece the lamb."

"My sister and Miss Colby, since you appear so interested in their welfare, are both at home with the headache," said Lord Hawksborough, turning away.

"They're both at Frederica Mannering's faro table," cackled Mrs. Burke, "or I'll eat my wig."

Lady Mary was performing a neat *entrechat* in a set of the quadrille when she stumbled and almost fell. She had just seen Lord Hawksborough striding out of the ballroom with a face like thunder.

She contained herself as best she could until the dance was over. Mrs. Burke came up immediately. "I was talking to Hawksborough," she began.

"Where *is* Charles?" demanded Lady Mary, looking at Mrs. Burke with dislike.

"Said he had to find that Colby girl," said Mrs. Burke maliciously, watching with satisfaction the red tide of anger rising in Lady Mary's face.

"Is that the sister of the Colby I met at Bellingham?" said Betty Barrington, stopping suddenly beside them. "I had such hopes of Richard Colby. I met him when I was at the seminary in Bellingham, you know, I sent him to get chocolate drops. Well, he wanted to know when the Hawksborough coach was leaving, and that was on the very day they were held up by highwaymen. I thought Mr. Colby was a dashing and romantic highwayman who would throw me over his saddle bow and ride off with me. But alas! It was all so ordinary. I met him at a ball and he turned out to be nothing more than a respectable young man who had a *tendre* for Susan Fitzgerald. Ah, me!" said Betty, rolling her eyes in mock distress. "My heart was quite broken!"

She flitted off. Mrs. Burke saw new prey and took herself off as well.

Lady Mary stood very still, her blue eyes quite, quite blank.

Amanda had at last succeeded in dragging a reluctant Susan back to Lady Mannering's in Montague Street. Susan was in a foul temper. The supper was in the form of a buffet and Susan immediately left Amanda to her card-playing and stomped over to it and began to help herself to an amazing amount of delicacies, which she proceeded to wash down with several bumpers of claret.

Drawing room and back drawing room had been joined together for the added company. There was hardly any sound, apart from occasional voices making a bid. Amanda was immediately and totally absorbed in the game.

She lost a little and won a little, just as she done on the night before. And then she began to lose steadily.

At one point she raised anguished eyes from her cards and looked to where Susan was moodily drinking wine.

Susan caught the look and came over and stood beside her. As Amanda's last guineas were scooped away, Susan leaned over the banker's muslin shoulder and ran a thumb over the cards.

"No wonder you're losing," she said in a loud carrying voice she had inherited from her mother. "These cards are marked. See!" She held one up to the room full of women. "Pinpricks. The oldest trick in the game."

"Cheat!" raged Amanda, seeing Fox End and an escape from Lord Hawksborough and the terrors of the London Season being snatched from her.

"Nonsense," said Lady Mannering, sweeping forward regally. "Do not listen to the silly words of these little misses. Murphy! See these ladies leave immediately."

A large, tough individual who acted as butler lumbered forward purposely.

"Give her her money back," said Susan, her eyes glittering with wine and excitement, "or I'll draw your cork."

"I wouldn't like to see the pretty ladies gettin' their darlin' faces messed up, now, would I?" said Murphy with awful geniality.

There was a fluttering in the room. Feathers on headdresses trembled, reticules were hurriedly scooped up, chairs were pushed back.

Murphy swung around. "Now, ladies," he said. "You will just all be keepin' to your seats until this little matter is sorted out."

He squared his massive shoulders under his plush jacket and the ladies nervously subsided—with the exception of Amanda and Susan.

Amanda marched up to him and put her hands on her hips. "My money," she demanded loudly, "or I will summon the watch."

Murphy picked her up and twisted her round so that she was held powerless against him.

"I'll just be putting this bit o' rubbish outside where it belongs, my lady," he said to Lady Mannering.

"Stop!"

Susan marched forward and faced Murphy. Her black eyes were fixed on him in an autocratic glare of great hauteur. Her voice had a cutting edge, and she said, "Release her this instant!"

And Murphy did as he was bid, almost unconsciously reacting to the edge of authority in Susan's voice.

"You *fool*, Murphy," hissed Lady Mannering.

Murphy hesitated and began to advance on Amanda again.

Amanda, who had skipped quickly out of his reach as soon as she was released, walked over to Lady Mannering and faced up to her, her little jaw thrust out.

"My money," she said slowly and clearly. "You will give me my money . . . you . . . you . . . horrible old Friday-faced *cheat*!"

"I have no intention of giving you a single penny," retorted Lady Mannering coolly. "Murphy, remove these creatures."

"These ladies will not let you treat us thus," said Amanda, looking confidently around the room for help. But the ladies who frequent gaming hells do not cultivate notoriety of any sort. Eyes stared at the floor, at the ceiling, at anywhere except at Amanda and Susan.

"If my husband learns of this," whispered one lady to another in Amanda's hearing, "I will be sent to the country to rusticate!"

Murphy glanced around the room. He saw that no one was going to come to the help of the girls.

He advanced again on Amanda.

Susan edged close to Amanda. "We must summon the watch," she whispered urgently. "Try to keep everyone's attention on you."

Amanda faced Murphy. "Lord Hawksborough will be here at any moment," she cried.

Murphy hesitated.

"Go on," snapped Lady Mannering. "No one knows these girls are here! Do you think they would have been allowed out without a maid? Get rid of them, Murphy. There is no need to be gentle. They dare not tell anyone where they have been."

Out of the corner of her eye Amanda saw Susan edging towards the buffet. For one despairing moment Amanda thought Susan was calmly going to start eating again. Hoping that Susan really *had* some plan of action, Amanda pointed to the doorway. "Look!" she cried. "*There* is his lordship!"

Murphy swung round, Lady Mannering opened her mouth to shout to him that Amanda was lying, and in that second Susan picked up a pitcher of ice water and threw the contents full at the blazing chandelier.

The effect on the company was the same as the effect Tam o' Shanter had on the witches in the kirk when he called out "Weel done, Cutty-Sark!" In an instant, all was dark. Figures scrambled through the gloom. Women screamed and fought for the door.

"My money," wailed Amanda.

Susan threw up window. "Help!" she screamed in a loud voice. "Help! Summon the watch!"

In the dim light of the back drawing room, which was lit by only one oil lamp, Amanda saw Lady

Mannering wrenching at a door, trying to make her escape.

"She's getting away," she shouted to Susan.

She ran into the back drawing room with Susan at her heels. Lady Mannering popped a fat purse down her cleavage and stood glaring.

"Doxy! Jade! Whore!" hissed Lady Mannering.

"Where's the money?" demanded Susan.

"I have not got any money," snarled Lady Mannering. "Let me go!"

"She put a purse down her gown," gasped Amanda, holding tightly onto Lady Mannering by her arms.

"Then let's shake her down," said Susan cheerfully.

The light from several newly lit candles sprang up in the drawing room behind them, but they were too engrossed to turn around.

And that was how Lord Hawksborough found his sister and Miss Amanda Colby. Both of them were furiously shaking a middle-aged lady until her teeth rattled.

"What on earth do you think you are doing?" demanded Lord Hawksborough. "Desist this minute."

A large purse fell from under Lady Mannering's skirts and Amanda scooped it up.

"Charles," she gasped, swinging around. "We must leave. I promise I will explain."

The rattle of the watch sounded from the end of the street. Lady Mannering succeeded in opening the door she had tried to open earlier and slammed and bolted it behind her.

Lord Hawksborough grabbed both girls by the upper arms and bustled them out into the street and into his carriage.

He seized the reins and set off down the street at a sedate trot. The watch shouted something and Lord Hawksborough reined in.

" 'Evening melord," said the watch. "Wot's all this about shouting and screaming down this 'ere street?"

"I do not know," said Lord Hawksborough politely. "But there is a house a little back with its front door lying open, and there seemed to be a deal of commotion going on inside."

The watchman touched his hat and set off at a trot.

Susan collapsed in helpless giggles. "How clever of you, Charles," she said at last. "I declare I have never had so much fun in my life. You should have heard Amanda call Lady Mannering a horrible Friday-faced cheat. Better than the Haymarket, it was!"

"You will both maintain a decorous silence until we reach home," he snapped, springing his horses. "I hope no one reports you to the authorities. Was there anyone left, apart from Lady Mannering?"

"No," said Amanda, dreading the row she knew was coming. "They all ran away. An awful bruiser called Murphy ran away too, the minute Susan called for the watch."

"I told you to be quiet," he said in a voice now held well in check. "Please do as I command."

"Then don't ask questions," said Amanda crossly.

He glared at her and set his mouth in a firm line.

Susan was still chortling to herself, but even she sobered as they reached the mansion in Berkeley Square. She at last realised her brother was very angry indeed.

He led them into a small, little-used morning room, wanting to find out all about it before Lady Mary arrived home with his mother and Aunt Matilda.

The room was chilly. Amanda remembered they had both left their cloaks at the house in Montague Street.

The room was in shades of gold and yellow. There were some fine pictures, pretty gilt chairs, and a case of pretty figurines against one wall, but it smelled slightly of damp.

Lord Hawksborough took up a position in front of the fireplace and said wrathfully, "Now, begin at the beginning and go on to the end. Not you, Susan. I wish Miss Colby to explain, first, what she was doing in a gaming house, and second, what the devil she meant by inducing my sister to go with her."

Amanda felt drained of all emotion. She told him in a tired voice of how she had wished to make money so that she and Richard and Aunt Matilda could return to the country, so that she would not be plagued with trying to find a husband.

She told him of Susan finding the marked cards and of the melee that had ensued.

Lord Hawksborough turned eyes like steel on his sister. "I had thought you were beginning to show some sense, Susan. Of late, you have shown a certain elegance and good breeding. It began to appear that your popularity was not based on an eccentric whim of fashion but on the fact that you had appeared to be developing an attractive personality." Susan flushed with pleasure.

"However," went on her brother sternly, "you show that you have more hair than wit. A gambling hell! And of the worst sort. The mischief these places do is almost incalculable; bankruptcies, embezzlements, duels, and suicides."

"Pooh!" said Susan unrepentantly. "It's just as well I

did go along. You should have seen Lady Mannering's face when I called out the cards were marked. Famous!"

"I am very angry," said Lord Hawksborough. "Miss Colby, if you must gamble, at least go to a respectable establishment. How on earth did you find out about Lady Mannering?"

"Lady Mary had an invitation," said Amanda. "She did not ask for it back, and so I decided to use it. She said these gaming houses were genteel, and I *did* see various society ladies that I know."

"*Any* gaming house that would allow two unchaperoned misses entrance is one of ill repute. I am surprised at your naiveté. You must have misunderstood Lady Mary. And how did you get there? I saw no carriage."

"In a hack," said Susan grumpily. For all her faults, Susan would never have dreamt of betraying a servant, and she knew the coachman had been waiting in a tavern around the corner.

Susan stood up abruptly. "It's all very well for you to go on like a jaw-me-dead, Charles, but Amanda said if she got enough money then I could go with her to that place, Fox End, and not have to go to balls and parties. I think Amanda and I were very resourceful and brave. So it's no use you glaring at me. I don't see why you and Mama should sport the blunt for a Season when you've got two females on your hands who want none of it.

"I'm off to bed, Charles. I have drunk so much bad wine, I have a rumpus among my chitterlings."

Susan strode to the door, wrenched it open, and banged it shut behind her with such force that the little figurines wobbled and shook in their glass case.

"You see?" demanded Lord Hawksborough. "That girl is rowdy and graceless and . . ."

"And very resourceful and brave, as she pointed out," said Amanda quietly. "I shudder to think of my humiliation had she not been with me. It was quick-witted of her to . . . to th-throw that g-great j-jug of ice w-water at the chandelier."

"Do not cry," said the viscount in a gentle voice.

"I'm not crying, I'm laughing," wailed Amanda. "Oh, it all seems so very funny *now*."

He glared down at her and then gave a reluctant grin. "I confess I was startled out of my wits when I arrived, to find you and Susan shaking the life out of Lady Mannering."

"Will it cause a great scandal?"

He shook his head. "I doubt very much if any of the ladies would dare say they had been there."

"But why do they go? Why go to be cheated?"

"Because they are mostly inveterate gamblers. Lady Mannering makes sure they win a great deal on the first visit, provided she is sure they will come back again. On the second visit, they lose. Lady Mannering kindly offers them an IOU so that they may go on playing. Usually, some unfortunate accepts. She loses again, but then she is in debt to Lady Mannering, and so must return to clear her losses . . . which she never does. Lady Mannering threatens to expose her, and the lady raises it somehow by crying to her husband or pawning some of her jewels.

"Now, tell me, what exactly did Lady Mary say?"

"She . . . she has been pleasant to me of late. I told her I wished to find money somehow so that I could leave London.

"She laughed and told me about these gaming houses for women. Then she showed me Lady Mannering's card. She thought she heard you arriving, so she left the room, and left me still holding the card."

Lord Hawksborough looked very grim, and he swung around and stared down at the empty fireplace.

Amanda cleared her throat nervously. "I think Lady Mary was not malicious in her intent."

"I think she was," he said flatly. "I can understand her reasons, but she has gone too far."

And yet you will marry her, thought Amanda sadly.

"Leave Amanda," he said in a low voice. "I might forget myself again."

She moved sadly towards the door.

"Amanda!"

He had swung round and was standing erect in front of the fireplace. He looked steadily at her, and what she saw in his eyes made her catch her breath.

"I must release myself from this engagement," he said. "When that is achieved, we will discuss matters. Do you understand?"

She nodded dumbly, a great happiness filling her.

He walked to the door and held it open for her and stood looking down at her. Lady Mary had already arrived home and was standing by the door of the Red Drawing Room, across the hall in the shadows. Neither Lord Hawksborough nor Amanda saw her.

Lord Hawksborough took Amanda's hand and raised it to his lips, and she shyly put up her hand and caressed the wings of black hair above his forehead.

"Go," he said softly. "Until tomorrow."

"Until tomorrow," echoed Amanda.

Lady Mary slid back into the Red Drawing Room and stood with her back to the door, her bosom heaving.

Mrs. Fitzgerald looked at her curiously. "Is anything the matter? You look upset."

"No, nothing," said Lady Mary. "Nothing at all."

She calmly walked over to the tea tray and picked up her cup. Lady Mary had become an almost permanent guest in Berkeley Square. She had already begun to look on the mansion as her own.

Now all this was to be snatched from her by a common country miss with a face like a fox.

Lady Mary knew instinctively, after the scene she had just witnessed, that Charles would make a push to escape from his engagement at the first opportunity.

To be jilted again!

9

Amanda awoke to a glittering day full of dappled sunlight and the sound of rushing wind. She and Susan went off early for their morning ride, laughing and joking and more at ease with each other than they had ever been before.

The money taken back from Lady Mannering had amounted to eight hundred guineas. After a long debate with her conscience, Amanda had returned three hundred guineas by messenger, for she knew that she and Susan had temporarily destroyed Lady Mannering's source of income.

In vain did Susan point out that Amanda would probably have won that sum had the cards not been marked. But Amanda had decided she did not want to take money she was sure was not rightfully hers.

There was only one dark shadow on the sunshine of her morning.

As she was standing with Susan in the hall, she sensed a thrill of menace in the air.

Instinctively she turned and looked up at the first landing.

Lady Mary was standing there, her hand clutching the banister so tightly the knuckles showed white. Her eyes were filled with naked hatred. Amanda shuddered and turned away.

But the day outside was fresh and warm and windy, so that her feelings of fear and guilt quickly left her. Even the sight of the stocky figure of Townsend, the Bow Street Runner, heading around Berkeley Square, the sun sparkling from the crown on top of his baton, did not damp her sudden lift of spirits.

The jewels had been returned. Surely Charles had grown tired of searching for the highwaymen. He had vowed vengeance, but that had been some time ago.

Lady Mary saw the Runner being ushered into the library and quickly followed him in. She knew Mr. Townsend never stayed very long.

That would give her an opportunity to play on Charles's feelings of honour, so that he would realise that he could not break the engagement.

Charles looked up at her, his eyes veiled. He rose punctiliously to his feet, waited until she was seated, and then sat down again and turned back to Mr. Townsend, who was sitting opposite.

"Go on, Mr. Townsend," said Lord Hawksborough. "You were saying you returned to Bellingham and Hember Cross."

"Yes, my lord, I had gone through the name of every kiddey that was ever chaunted for a toby," said Mr. Townsend, meaning that he had studied the name of every felon whose name had been published in the newspapers in connection with highway robbery. "And the more I reads, the more I comes to the conclusion that there's amateurs behind this.

"Now, there's this house called Fox End . . ."

Lord Hawksborough's eyes went quite blank and Lady Mary leaned forward slightly in her chair.

"It's precious near where the robbery took place, and local report says the people there have a donkey and a horse. Now, I found an old gent resident there who says he's letting the house from respectable people. 'Who's the donkey belong of?' I asked. 'A werry 'spectable young lady,' says he.

"So that's that, I thinks. Then I sees in the pasture beyond the house, a bully-fellow striding up and down and slashing bits off the hedge with his stick.

" 'Who's that?' I asks. 'That,' says the old gent, 'is a dreadful man called Brotherington. I have managed to make his life just as unpleasant for him as he has made everyone else's, and if he don't stop cutting that hedge, I'll have him back in court.'

" 'I'll tell him,' I says, having found, my lord, that a sore and angry man is a great source of information. So I outs and speaks to this Brotherington. Well, I find the name of the owners of the horse and donkey are Miss and Master Colby and that's the lady and gentleman who are staying here, and so I was about to give up and go away.

"Suddenly this Brotherington, he says, 'Waren't there a report that them highwaymen was wearing wigs and masks?'

" 'Yes, black or red wigs,' says I, your lordship not being sure, what with it being dark. There's the remains of this bonfire on t'other side of the hedge in the garden of Fox End, and this Brotherington leans over and points with his stick. I lean over the hedge and this is what I find."

He picked up a canvas roll from beside his chair and slowly opened it and spread it out on the table.

Lying on the canvas were various charred and blackened objects. They had not burned completely. Three strands of bright red wool adhering to a piece of canvas were pointed out by Mr. Townsend's stubby finger. Also, an edge of a mask with the ribbon still complete, and one charred and blackened tricorne.

Lady Mary held her breath. All at once she remembered Betty Barrington saying that Richard had called at the seminary at Bellingham to find out at what time the Hawksborough coach was leaving for London.

Lord Hawksborough suddenly smiled. "Well done, Townsend. You have worked hard. But I fear you are on the wrong scent. Give me a day to think about this. It was not, of course, the Colbys. They would never do such a thing. But this Brotherington may have found these objects elsewhere and placed them in the garden at Fox End out of spite. Perhaps I shall send you back to question him further. Miss Colby is a young and gently reared lady. You have met her yourself. She is totally incapable of such an act."

But, almost unbidden, a picture of Amanda ruthlessly shaking Lady Mannering sprang into his mind.

Lady Mary slipped quietly from the room.

Lord Hawksborough had failed to tell her the jewels had been returned. He had told his mother, Susan, and Aunt Matilda, but he had been so busy explaining away to Lady Mary his strange behaviour with respect to Amanda on the night the jewels were returned that he had forgotten to tell her about the recovery.

Lady Mary was on her way to search Amanda's room. One jewel would be enough, she thought savagely.

Miss Amanda did not have any jewellery at all, so the presence of just one jewel somewhere in her room would be proof enough.

She quietly pushed open the door of Amanda's room. Quickly she began to search. Finally she began to tear everything apart. She slit the lining of cloaks and pelisses, she ripped open the pillows so that feathers flew about the room like a snowstorm, but not one single jewel did she manage to unearth. She looked around the wreckage of the room, clenching and unclenching her hands in desperation. She *must* find evidence or her violent search of the room would be regarded as mere spite.

The curtains fluttered in the wind and a dancing sunbeam flickered over the top of the tallboy.

With an exclamation, Lady Mary dragged over a chair and stood on it, her fingers searching the top of the tallboy.

Her first feeling when she found only a book was one of intense disappointment. But she opened it anyway. A diary! A pulse of excitement began to beat at her throat as she quickly turned the pages.

The recent pages contained only an occasional sentence: "Today I went to supper at Lady A's," " This evening, went to the opera," and so on.

But earlier in the diary, there was one full page of writing. Lady Mary sat down to read, and as she read, she began to experience a sweet feeling of triumph. It was all there. All Amanda's guilt and worry about the robbery, and her hopes that Richard would be able to restore the jewels.

She hurried back into the library, clutching the diary.

Lord Hawksborough rose to his feet and looked at her gravely.

"I am glad you have come, Mary," he said in a gentle voice. "Sit down. What I am about to say—"

"Read this first!" cried Lady Mary, fumbling open the pages of the diary until she found the incriminating one.

He frowned at her, but, seeing her excitement, he sat down and began to read.

At last he looked up, his face grim and hard. "So it was them after all," he said in a flat voice.

"It'll be transportation at least," said Lady Mary, her eyes bright with malice.

"I will handle this without the law."

"Oh, no, you won't," cried Lady Mary. "I shall take that diary to Bow Street."

With one abrupt move he hurled the diary into the fire, and held her back, as she would have snatched it out of the flames.

"I have been mistaken in the Colbys, Mary," he said in a cold voice, "and I have been equally mistaken in you. Your desire to expose Miss Colby to me was perfectly understandable in the circumstances. Your raging malice is not. I was . . . much taken with Miss Colby. It is a bitter fact to face that I do not understand women at all. This does not alter the decision I came to last night. In fact, it strengthens it. I cannot marry you, Mary."

"I'll sue you for breach of promise," she said viciously.

"Oh, Mary," he sighed, with an awful kind of pity. "To be jilted once was bad enough for your reputation. Screaming at me in the courts for wanting to behave in a similar way will ruin you. There is no need to sue me.

I am quite prepared to make you a handsome settlement. I am prepared to let the world think that you have jilted me."

"How much?" demanded Lady Mary flatly.

And in those two words, Lord Hawksborough saw with a sad wonder that she had never loved him.

"My lawyers will deal with the matter. Do not worry. I will be generous and my lawyers will be discreet."

"And you are going to let the Colbys get away with it? What about the jewels?"

"They returned them long ago. But, no, I am not going to let them escape unpunished. While I decide what to do, it would be better if you leave this house."

"I shall stay long enough to see the look on that minx's face when you tell her."

"Then you will be disappointed. For I shall not breathe a word until you are gone."

Lady Mary stormed to the door, but his voice stopped her. "Mary!" he said. "I would like to point out that you must not speak about this, or you will not receive *one penny* from me, and you can sue to kingdom come for all the good it may do you."

When she had gone, he sat for a long time looking at the fire.

Amanda sensed the uneasy atmosphere in the house as soon as she arrived back with Susan. She sat eating luncheon in the dining room with Susan, Aunt Matilda, and Mrs. Fitzgerald. She had gone to Susan's room to wash and comb her hair and chat, since Mrs. Fitzgerald said there was no need to change their dress for an informal family meal.

And so Amanda did not see the wreckage of her room or know that the diary was missing.

At one point during the meal, Lord Hawksborough strode in. He did not look at Amanda, but addressed his mother direct. "I want you all to stay at home until I send for you," he said harshly. "Do not go out."

"But Charles," protested Mrs. Fitzgerald, "we were to call on—"

"I said *do not go out of this house!*"

He swung on his heel and marched out.

"What on earth . . ." began Mrs. Fitzgerald.

Susan ran to the window and looked out. "Mary is leaving," she cried. "All her trunks are being put in the coach."

Amanda lowered her eyes. Her feeling of elation was mixed with guilt. What if Lady Mary had really loved Charles! But then excitement and anticipation took over. Soon he would propose. She would be married to the man she loved.

Perhaps one day she might even have the courage to tell him about the robbery.

But her feeling of happiness began to fade. Mrs. Fitzgerald kept saying she had never known Charles to be so upset or so testy. And then, even with the departure of Lady Mary, the air seemed thick with tension and unease.

Then Lord Hawksborough threw open the door of the dining room. This time his eyes fastened on Amanda. "Miss Colby, come with me," he snapped, and without waiting for her answer, he turned on his heel and marched into the hall.

"You had better see what Charles wants," sighed Mrs. Fitzgerald. "But count on't that it's only his spleen that is disordered."

Amanda hurried out into the hall.

Lord Hawksborough kept his back to her and addressed the front door. "We are going driving, Miss Colby. Now!"

"Perhaps I should change," volunteered Amanda breathlessly.

"No, you will do as you are." He opened the door and stood aside to let her pass.

For a brief moment their eyes met, and Amanda's fell before the steel-cold contempt in his.

Frightened, she said, "Perhaps Susan would—"

"What I have to say to you, Miss Colby," he said in measured tones, "is something I do not wish overheard by *anyone*."

The jewels! thought Amanda in sudden blind panic. He has found out we took the jewels.

She simply nodded and climbed into his curricle and stared straight ahead while he picked up the reins.

Numb with misery, Amanda was only vaguely aware of the passing houses. They went up to Oxford Street, then along High Holborn, and turned off at Gray's Inn Road. He is taking me into the country to wring my neck, thought Amanda with a sort of miserable satisfaction.

All the long length of Gray's Inn Road, she tried to find her voice, tried to speak, but each time the grim set of his face made all her courage melt away.

He stopped at last outside the Angel at Islington, which, despite the growth of the suburb, still presented the appearance of an old-fashioned country inn, with its double galleries in the yard supported by columns and carved pilasters with caryatids.

He called to an ostler to hold the reins, sprang down, and vanished inside.

He was back a few minutes later, saying, "I have bespoke a private parlour. We will not be disturbed."

The ostler leered, and got such a savage look from his lordship that he changed the leer quickly into a sycophantic grin.

Amanda allowed herself to be helped down.

All the way upstairs to the private parlour, she watched the rigid set of his shoulders and wondered why she could not find the courage to flee.

Once they were inside, he turned the key in the door.

"How did you find out?" asked Amanda through white lips.

"Oh, the devil take it!" he said, tossing his hat on the table and running his hands through his hair. "All the way here, I was praying I had been mistaken. I was praying that that diary was not yours but merely a forgery on the part of Lady Mary. But the first words out of your mouth condemn you. Why did you do it?"

"I . . . we . . . needed the money."

"Money!" he ground out savagely. "Is there no such thing in the whole wide world left like the honest love of one woman for one man? Are you all harpies? Lady Mary turned out to want only my wealth. But at least she did not hold me up at gunpoint to get it!"

"We hardly knew you," choked out Amanda. "You do not know what it is like to be poor and—"

He ruthlessly cut across her faltering words, his voice

acid with contempt. "Had the pair of you been two waifs from some thieves' kitchen who had never known the decencies of life, then I would have forgiven you. Your brother is young and strong. Did it never occur to you to make shift and find work? No, of course it didn't. There's bad blood in the pair of you. You are not only immoral, you are *amoral*. Do you know, if my mother's elderly coachman had not spoiled my aim, I could have *killed* you? Do you not realise if she had elected to travel with any other than those aged servants she regards as pets, you would be in a pit of quicklime by now?

"The sheer immoral folly . . . the sheer selfishness of it. But by the time you and your brother found yourselves in my well-feathered nest, you realised there was no need to keep the jewels. Not when you could have the lot. Not when you, you doxy, could entrap me.

"I accepted your explanation for stealing your aunt's beau. And Susan's, I may add. I should have listened to the voice of my common sense, which might have told me you were nothing more than a grubby adventuress.

"Yes, a *harpy*, thoughtless of anyone else's feelings, using me, your aunt, my mother, and Susan as if we were so many chess pieces. Well, checkmate, Amanda."

"What will you do with me?" asked Amanda through white lips.

"Aye, there's the rub. Do with you?" He gave a harsh laugh. "I can't do anything with you, you jade. To tell the truth at home would kill your aunt and distress my mother beyond reason. But there is one thing I can do to keep a contamination like yourself away from my family. I have a friend who is a physician. He will diagnose a highly dangerous and infectious

disease planned to last to the end of the Season. You
will stay confined in your room, seeing no one."

"And Richard?" said Amanda, putting a hand to her
head, which felt burning hot.

"Young Colby will be sent to sea. It will be years
before you see him again."

"Oh, God, if you would only listen, only understand!"
cried Amanda.

"You will do as you are told," he said in a hard
voice. "If you do not, you will be transported to Botany
Bay and your brother will hang."

He seized his hat and crammed it on his head. He
grasped her roughly by the arm, and unlocking the
door with his free hand, bundled her roughly down the
stairs.

Amanda cried dismally the whole long journey home.
When they arrived at Berkeley Square, he looked at her
woebegone face with bitter satisfaction.

"Good. You look ill," he said. "Go straight to your
room and let me make your excuses to my mother and
your aunt. Then I will send for young Colby."

Amanda fled to her room. Although a squad of
housemaids had put everything to rights, she could see
it had been searched. The diary was gone, and all her
belongings were in different positions. She was now
beyond tears. The clothes, which had had their linings
slit, were lying in a neat pile, ready for repair. She felt
cold and sick. He would never understand that it was
two romantic children who had planned the highway
robbery. Two children who had been humiliated
so much at the assembly that he had seemed fair
game.

Two children who had grown up too late.

There came an urgent scratching at the door. "It's me, Susan. Open the door."

Wearily Amanda walked across the room and tried the handle. But of course! Lord Hawksborough had locked her in.

"I can't, Susan," she whispered back, her mouth close to the panels. "It's locked."

"Wait! Oh, the key's on *this* side of the door." There was a click as the lock opened and Susan strode into the room.

"Look here, Amanda," she said gruffly. "I called on Lady Mary because I wondered why she had left without saying good-bye. She said Charles was not marrying her because of you. I said you were a trump and it was all ridiculous. She told me to ask you. So here I am."

Amanda was all at once overcome with the desire to unburden her woes to a friend. And so she told Susan the whole story of the highway robbery and of Lady Mary finding the diary.

"You must help me explain to Charles," ended Amanda. "You must get him to understand—"

"I can only get him to understand what *I* understand," said Susan harshly. "You are a common, greedy little thief. I agree it should be kept from Mama and your aunt. But I wish you *had* an infectious disease. You *are* an infection, a veritable pox! As for Richard Colby . . ." Susan's voice cracked and large tears began to roll down her face. "I had thought . . . had hoped . . . Oh, what does it matter now. Mama is right. 'There will be plenty of suitors gathered round your dowry,' she said. I wish I were dead. I hope Richard goes to sea, and I hope . . . I hope they *keel-haul* him!"

She fled from the room and locked the door behind her.

Amanda sat very still. Now she had the guilt of Susan's grief to add to the other guilt. Poor Susan, whose very fragile self-esteem, whose newfound confidence, had been smashed by the thought that Richard only wanted her money. Why else would a thief and a highwayman be interested in her?

Amanda rose stiffly and walked to the window and looked out. An open carriage was turning the square with two elaborately dressed ladies holding parasols over their heads. One of them dipped her lace parasol. It was Miss Devine. For a moment it seemed as if she looked full at Amanda. Then she raised her parasol and the carriage bowled past.

Amanda drew in a deep shuddering breath. Miss Devine brought back vividly the assembly at Hember Cross, where it all seemed to have begun.

But at the bottom of her misery a little spark of anger was beginning to burn. What did any of these people know of the fear of poverty? If one had been brought up to assume that members of one's class never worked, then how was one supposed to *think* of work?

We should have stayed at Fox End and turned the whole garden over to vegetables and kept geese and chickens, thought Amanda.

But we had no one sensible to advise us. We never thought for a moment that Aunt Matilda would make some shift to help us out of trouble.

She turned as the lock clicked in the door again. A tray was pushed into the room by means of a long pole. The scared face of a servant briefly appeared in the doorway, and then the door was slammed and locked.

It appeared as if the tale of her severe infectious disease was already all over the house.

Amanda was amazed to find she was very hungry despite her misery. After she had eaten a good meal and drunk two glasses of claret, she began to search around in her mind for a way out of her predicament. It was all right for herself—well, not all right, but not as bad as poor Richard, faced with years at sea.

Amanda sat up very straight. Somehow, she had to get to Oxford before he left and warn him. She had the five-hundred guineas.

But how to get out of the room?

She sat all day puzzling over it, until she felt she had hit on a sort of plan. She ate her evening meal and then settled down to wait until the whole house was asleep.

She began to feel tired and wondered whether to try to catch a few hours' sleep herself, but dreaded the idea of waking up and finding it morning.

Amanda waited and waited until the clock on the mantel chimed three silvery notes and the hoarse-voiced watch in the square outside called three o'clock in the morning and added it was a fine starlit night.

She took a bodkin from her dressing table, slid a sheet of paper halfway under the door, and poked and fiddled, trying to make the key fall onto the paper so that she could draw it underneath the door to her side.

At first she was too anxious, too nervous, and her hands perspired so much that the bodkin kept slipping in her grasp. At last she took a deep breath and forced herself to concentrate on her task.

After what seemed a very long time, the key suddenly fell with a satisfying plop on the paper on the other side. Amanda drew it under the door with trembling hands.

Now, to escape!

She made her preparations carefully, packing up only two handboxes full of clothes. She put on a wool gown and a warm cloak and then took a deep breath and let herself out into the passageway.

Very carefully, frightened to make a sound, she made her way down to the back entrance that John the coachman had shown her. Once down the passageway beside the mews, she stopped and waited for the mad thumping of her heart to subside.

She had done it! Now to warn Richard.

But the early-morning stage to Oxford turned out to be fully booked, and she had to wait impatiently until eight-twenty in the evening, which was when the Oxford Mail took the road.

The day had turned very warm and she was hot and tired and dusty by the time she climbed aboard the coach at The Swan with Two Necks in Lad Lane. She settled back in her seat with a sigh of relief, feeling some of the tension easing from her body.

The Royal Mail coaches were still regarded as a miracle of speed and Amanda stared wide-eyed at the timetable posted outside the inn:

London—Edinburgh	(400 miles)	45½ hours
London—York	(197 miles)	20 hours
London—Manchester	(185 miles)	19 hours

Imagine being in Scotland in a mere 45½ hours! The world was shrinking in an exciting way, thought

Amanda. To be able to see all those faraway places, to have them brought magically within reach.

The Royal Mail kept to a strict timetable. The mail guards on the coaches carried a sealed watch and a timetable, which was handed on from one to the other. It gave the precise schedule for the journey, and it was the mail guard's task to see that any delay in starting was made up during the journey to the next stage.

Riding the mail coach was still considered quite a daring thing to do, although the timid Aunt Matilda had somehow taken it in her stride. There were many stories of people who had died from fright when the coach went over fifteen miles an hour, and many a physician learnedly explained that the celerity would give rise to an affection of the brain.

The mail coaches were all the same design, painted maroon and black, and built in the Millbank yard by a man called Vidler.

The mail guard was the only Post Office figure on the coach and he was an imposing sight. His coat was scarlet with blue lapels and white ruffles.

His coat lining of blue matched the blue of his heavy cloth waistcoat. He wore nankeen breeches and white silk stockings, and his hat had a gold band on it. The curved bugle of Elizabethan days, although still used as the insignia of the Posts, had given way to a long brass horn on which the guard could play his own composition, so that every innkeeper, every stableboy, and every turnpike guard would know who was in charge of the mail that day.

At eight-twenty precisely, the many-caped coachman up on the box shouted to the guard at the back, "All right behind?"

"All right," came the reply.

"Off she goes!" cried the coachman.

The guard blew an elaborate fanfare on his horn as the mail coach surged forward. Then he put his instrument away in a little tunnel of a basket fastened to the coach side and began to ask everyone on the roof his destination.

Inside the coach, in all the luxury of a comfortable seat, Amanda said farewell to London.

Her eyes filled with tears as the City streets fled past, until London wavered like a drowned metropolis in front of her.

At last, weary with emotion and heat and fatigue, she fell asleep.

The Mail took only a mere six hours to reach Oxford, depositing Amanda in the middle of that city at two-twenty in the morning. She decided to put up for the rest of the night at the Gold Lion, and visit Richard at his college as soon as daylight arrived.

But standing in the innyard, a portmanteau beside him, waiting for the southbound Mail, was Richard.

Amanda screamed his name, and, racing across the yard, flung herself on his chest, crying, "Oh, you're safe. He has not sent you away!"

"Quiet down, Amanda," said Richard, pushing her a little away so that he could look at her. "A groom arrived not so long ago, waking up the whole college with the news that I was summoned to London by Lord Hawksborough immediately.

"Hawksborough has so many carriages. He has his own travelling carriage and then there's that antique thing of his mother's that we held up. I thought he might have sent one . . . Why, Amanda! You are shaking."

"He knows about the robbery, Richard. He . . . he said he could not turn us over to the law because of Aunt and his family, but . . . Oh, Richard, I am to be locked in my room until the end of the Season, and you are to be sent to sea for years and years and *years*." Here Amanda burst into noisy tears while Richard looked at her in horror. They were gradually collecting a small audience, and one blood strongly advised Richard to "marry the girl and do the gentlemanly thing."

"Here!" said Richard. "You'd best come into the inn and tell me all about it."

Like all posting inns, the Gold Lion was as busy in the middle of the night as it was during the day.

Soon they were seated over a bottle of wine. Richard's eyes grew wider and wider as Amanda told him the whole story.

"So you see," said Amanda, finished, "I cannot go back. I *had* to rescue you. I have five hundred guineas, Richard. Well, a bit less because of the coach fare. But we can both go back to Fox End and . . . and . . . dig over the garden and plant vegetables and keep chickens and . . ." Her voice trailed away before Richard's hard stare.

"No, Amanda," he said. "I'm going to face Hawksborough. He's not in love with *me*. Yes, you may stare! But that's the main reason you could not explain things properly to him. The man's in love with you. I noticed it a good while ago. You go to Fox End. A Mail goes from here to Hember Cross. Mr. Cartwright-Browne should have left. You stay there. If Lord Hawksborough still wants to send me to sea, then I'll need to take the punishment. We're lucky we didn't hang, Amanda. We did a pretty rotten thing and we're lucky to be alive."

A horn sounded from the yard.

"The Mail," said Richard, springing up. He gave Amanda a swift hug.

"Don't go," she said, clinging to him desperately.

"I must. You've had a hard time of it, sis, and it's my turn now."

A kiss on her cheek and he was gone.

Amanda sat back in her chair and buried her head in her hands.

They were paying for their crime. How long must they go on paying?

Richard wandered the streets of London for several hours, not quite knowing where he was going.

The day was sunny and still and warm, with only the faintest chill in the air to remind him of winter past.

He was determined to assemble all the facts and explanations in his head before he saw Lord Hawksborough.

He somehow had to explain that the highway robbery, which had seemed so reasonable, a sort of justified revenge, such a short time ago should now seem so wicked and childish. He was inhibited by the knowledge that Lord Hawksborough was in love with Amanda, a fact Richard found very strange. What such a man of the world could be doing falling for a chit like Amanda, thought Richard with affectionate brotherly contempt, was beyond his reasoning.

But what was even more inhibiting was his own feeling for Susan Fitzgerald. There was something about

Susan that always brought out the knight-errant in Richard. From first thinking her a decent sort of a girl when he had pretended to Betty Barrington that he had only gone to the seminary because he was in love with Susan, Richard's feelings had grown gradually warmer. Other girls were prettier, more feminine, but when Susan smiled, she seemed to light up the whole day. He had hoped shortly to ask her to wait for him, to wait until he finished his studies and found some position in life. Now all that was gone, and he had to fight not to feel bitter.

At last, after hours of walking, he decided the time had come to beard his lordship in his den. For the more he thought and worried about it, the more impossible the task seemed.

By the time he reached Berkeley Square, he was in a blue funk and could not help hoping Lord Hawksborough was not at home.

But his heart sank when the butler said his lordship was in the library and waiting for Mr. Colby. He had instructions to show Mr. Colby directly to his lordship the moment Richard arrived.

Richard slowly mounted the stairs, feeling as if he were mounting them on his knees.

Finally he was face to face with Lord Hawksborough. His lordship looked tired and grim. He was wearing an embroidered cambric shirt, leather breeches, and hessians. His shirt was open at the neck and somehow his casual dress made him appear less approachable than his usual impeccable formal wear.

His eyes were flat and cold and he raked Richard from head to toe with a contemptuous glance.

Richard broke the silence. "You found we took the jewels," he said.

"Like your sister, you seem to have guessed from the look on my face," said Lord Hawksborough. "Sit down!"

Richard sat down and laid his hat and cane on a nearby table. "I did not guess, my lord," he said. "Amanda told me."

"She told you! So *that's* where she went!"

"Well, don't you see, she felt she *had* to escape, to get away from you, because . . ." Richard quailed before the sudden blaze of fury in his lordship's eyes.

"But of course she did," said Lord Hawksborough sweetly. "Getting out of a locked room is as nothing to a girl who can hold up a coach."

"I know we did a dreadful thing. And I know that to say we are sorry is not enough," said Richard earnestly. "Hear me out . . . please."

Lord Hawksborough leaned back in his chair and studied Richard's face for a long moment, and then he nodded.

Richard took a deep breath and began. He talked for three-quarters of an hour and Lord Hawksborough did not interrupt him once.

Richard began with the death of their parents and with their upbringing by Aunt Matilda. He told him how they had lived on so little money that they had shunned social life, since social life would mean they had to buy clothes. He explained about the life he had led with Amanda, roaming the fields and woods, Amanda being more like a young brother than a girl.

Aunt Matilda, he said, had dinned into them the fact that the Colby's were gentry and of a higher class than Mr. Brotherington or even the vicar. They had come to think of their elevated social position as something very special, until they had begun to think themselves outside the normal laws of the land.

"I never knew Amanda was leading the life of a household drudge and that her only entertainment was following me around the countryside," Richard went on. "She never complained. She did not have any schooling, but that did not seem important, since she is only a girl. I never even thought of her marrying one day. I somehow thought we would always go on in the same way. Aunt Matilda did not give either of us much in the way of moral guidance."

Then he described the assembly. Vividly he recalled his humiliation at the hands of Miss Devine, and vividly he recounted it. He described their desperation, their need to find money. Amanda's description of what she thought was a great insult on the part of Lord Hawksborough had made them decide on the robbery.

It had seemed a game, said Richard. His voice sank as he told of their fear and shock when Amanda was nearly killed and of how they could not bear to look at the jewels. All they wanted to do was return them as soon as possible.

"Amanda is at Fox End," he said. "She did not try to escape your punishment for herself. She did not want me to be sent away to sea and took the Oxford Mail so that she could rescue me. But I told her that I would face you and take my punishment. It is different for girls. They get frightened easily. Amanda was shaking so much I thought she was going to break."

Lord Hawksborough half-turned his head away, and Richard said quickly, "I'm sorry, sir. I know you're in love with her . . . Oh, lor'."

"*How do you know?*" Lord Hawksborough stood up and looked down at Richard. The sun was behind him and his shadow fell across Richard's face so that Richard could not read his expression.

"Oh . . ." faltered Richard. "A certain something in the air between the two of you, so strong it was almost tangible. I found it hard to believe. Of course, I could understand *you* being in love, but it seemed funny Amanda being so lost and spoony. She had been such a hoyden only such a short time ago. I suppose brothers are intolerant, but it is a bit upsetting to see one's sister mooning around after another lady's fiancé. That sounds rude, but what I meant was— Where are you going, my lord?"

"Fox End," he said, striding to the door.

"But what about me? When would you like me to sign on?"

"Go back to Oxford, Colby."

"But, my lord, I must take my punishment!"

"Your punishment, Colby, will be to have me as a brother-in-law."

The door slammed. Richard, who had risen to his feet at Lord Hawksborough's departure, sat down again and cried in a most unmanly way out of sheer relief.

He finally dried his eyes, and helped himself to a glass of wine.

The door opened and Susan stood on the threshold, angry color rushing into her face as she saw him.

"Thief!" she screamed. "How *dare* you set foot in this house again?"

Richard marched over and picked her up in his arms and kissed her soundly. Then he plumped her down in a chair and sat opposite her. "You are going to listen to a story," he said, while Susan stared at him, her mouth hanging open. "It all began when our parents died. . . ."

Amanda sank down in a kitchen chair and gazed around at the lengthening shadows of evening. She had walked from the Mail to Fox End in the late afternoon, stopping at the vicarage to pick up the keys. She did not feel up to long explanations, and allowed Mrs. Jolly to think that her aunt and Richard were to follow by travelling carriage.

She had fed Bluebell, the donkey, and then Richard's horse. She had walked about the garden, planning where she would plant all sorts of useful vegetables.

Then she had saddled up Bluebell and ridden to Hember Cross to buy groceries, trying to parry a hundred questions from the townspeople and shopkeepers, the main one being: what was Miss Colby doing back so soon when they had all heard she would be in London for the Season?

Amanda murmured replies that her visit was temporary. She had merely come home after hearing of Mr. Cartwright-Browne's departure to make sure everything was in order. The townspeople had looked askance at her dusty dress and careworn appearance, but kept their dark thoughts to themselves.

Bluebell decided he wanted to go home as slowly as possible, stopping to look dreamily over hedges or crop grass, until Amanda dismounted and searched through a pannier of groceries to find the sugar loaves.

Once home, she had packed the groceries away and made herself a cold meal. The house seemed dark and silent.

Suddenly she felt nervous. The shadows began to seem threatening, and the once-familiar country noises, sinister.

She decided to light a fire in the morning room. As she crossed the hall, she nearly dropped her candle in fright as an owl hooted from the nearby woods.

Amanda lit the fire and sat back on her heels and watched the blaze.

So this is what her life was going to be like. Perhaps she would have to spend the rest of her days here alone, a shabby spinster, eating only what she could grow in the garden. Perhaps Aunt Matilda might learn after all of the robbery, and decide to stay forever with Mrs. Fitzgerald.

Amanda realized she had never lived alone before. She felt small and infinitely vulnerable. What if Mr. Brotherington should call and start to berate her?

Any thoughts of Lord Hawksborough had been kept at bay by the dash to Oxford and the return to Fox End. Now, all at once, she remembered the warmth and love in his eyes when he had said he would break his engagement.

Hot tears poured down Amanda's face. There was a sick, gnawing ache inside her and a terrible feeling of loss and mourning.

The sudden hard thud of hooves on the road outside, approaching at a great rate, made her cock her head and listen anxiously. The sound of galloping hooves came nearer and nearer, and then slowed, and then stopped.

And then she heard the banshee wail of the iron gates leading into the drive of Fox End being opened.

Almost immediately afterwards there was a great hammering on the door and a voice crying, "Amanda!"

Amanda slowly got to her feet, and then she gave a great sigh. It must be Richard.

Richard come home to say good-bye.

She rushed and opened the door.

The tall cloaked figure of Lord Hawksborough stood on the step.

"Oh, God!" said Amanda, reeling back, a hand to her lips.

" 'My lord' will do very well, Amanda," he said, walking past her into the hall.

Amanda led the way into the morning room.

She stood with her hands behind her back.

"My lord," she began, "I must try to explain—"

"Do not explain." He smiled. "Show me."

"Charles! You forgive me?"

"No, you must marry me as soon as possible. *That* is to be your punishment."

Amanda ran into his arms and buried her head against his chest.

"And Richard?" came her muffled voice.

"Back at Oxford."

"Oh, Charles, you are too good. I cannot marry you."

"You must. I did not bring a carriage. You have no chaperone. You are a fallen woman."

"You are only marrying me because you are sorry for me."

"I am not sorry for you in the slightest, my sweeting," said his lordship, pushing her chin up so that he could see her eyes. "I am sorry for myself. I cannot live without you."

He bent his head and kissed her long and lingeringly

with such tenderness and sweetness that Amanda began to cry again out of sheer happiness.

"I've never known such a watering pot," he murmured. "Will you cry the whole time?"

"No, I shall stop. You must have some refreshment, Charles. You must be famished."

"I am," he said, pulling her back into his arms and kissing her again.

"I did not mean *that* precisely," said Amanda when she could, giggling. "You make me feel quite *wanton*."

"I can do more than that," he said huskily, swinging off his cloak and throwing it over a chair. "Now," he said, his arms about her again, "where is that mouth of yours? I adore it as much as you admire my leg."

"Charles, how did you manage to forgive me?"

"Richard told me we were in love with each other."

"*Richard*! Richard cannot see beyond the end of his nose."

"What fond contempt you two have for each other! Oh, *Amanda* . . ."

He fell to kissing her again, at great length, and with such expertise that Amanda eventually broke a little away from him and whispered, "I do not mind if you stay the night, Charles."

"I am going out to stable my horse and I have every intention of staying the night. But not in your bed. No more eccentricities or irregularities. We will do the proper thing and wait for our wedding night, which will be just as soon as I can arrange it. Now, kiss me again."

Mr. Brotherington slowly backed away from the window of the morning room and went off home, shaking his head with gloomy satisfaction.

"Well, what did you find out, Papa?" asked his daughter, Priscilla.

"Just as I thought," he said.

Mr. Brotherington and Priscilla had heard reports in the town that Miss Colby had returned, looking ill and shabby. Curiosity had overcome him, and he had crept to look in the windows of Fox End, only to see Amanda Colby being ruthlessly kissed by a London swell.

"What happened?" nearly screamed Priscilla.

"She's gone to the bad, like I always said she would. There's no sign o' that aunt or brother o' hers, and they certainly didn't arrive in any travelling carriage like she said they would. I sneaked round by the stables and there's only the horse and donkey. But there's this great horse tethered outside. So I sees a light in one o' the downstairs windows and peeps in. And there's that wretched Amanda Colby being hugged and kissed by a London buck."

"Ooooh, Papa! Who was he?"

"Well, now you come to ask, it was that Lord Hawksborough, I think. And he don't mean marriage. Men don't, you know, when they go stark staring mad with passion like that. There's one blessing—that's something that will never happen to you, Priscilla. . . . Now, the Lord ha' mercy, what *have* I said to make you burst into tears?"

About the Author

Born in Glasgow, Scotland, Ms. Chesney started her writing career while working as a fiction buyer in a bookstore in Glasgow. She doubled as a theater critic, newspaper reporter, and editor before coming to the United States in 1971. Ms. Chesney lives with her husband and one child in New York.